CHRISTMAS BLITZ

AMY L. GALE

5 PRINCE PUBLISHING

Published by:

5 Prince Publishing and Books, LLC

DBA 5 Prince Publishing

PO Box 865

Arvada, Colorado 80001

Print ISBN: 978-1-63112-419-8

Interior design by 5 Prince Publishing

First Edition 2016

Second Edition 2025

For more information about this title, visit: www.5PrinceBooks.com

To my mom, Carol Riccetti,
who makes every Christmas magical

To my husband, Chris Gale,
who makes every day feel like Christmas.

Thank you for your unconditional love and support.

ACKNOWLEDGMENTS

I am enormously indebted to many wonderful people who have helped make Christmas Blitz a reality.

Chris Gale, my husband and favorite "Christmas Elf", who still makes sure Santa eats the cookies I leave out every Christmas Eve. You make every day feel like Christmas. Thank you for inspiring me and supporting my crazy dreams.

Carol Riccetti, my mother, who makes every Christmas magical and even sits on Santa's lap with me and Sadie (my Golden Retriever) for a Christmas picture. I'm blessed to have such a wonderful mother who truly believes I can do anything.

My "Girl's Book Club", Sharon, Rachel, and Kelly, who are constantly supporting and encouraging me to follow my dreams.

Ronnie Moran and Jeff Gazey, who helped me tremendously with the football portion of my story, and held in their laughter when I asked ridiculous questions.

My editor at 5 Prince Publishing, Cate Byers, who helped me polish my manuscript and offered great advice. I really enjoyed working with you.

Bernadette Marie, owner of 5 Prince Publishing, for putting together a wonder anthology with an amazing line up of authors.

Lisa J. Hobman, Railyn Stone, Susan Lohrer, Jessica Dall, and Bernadette, thank you for being a part of this project with me.

ALSO BY AMY L. GALE

CHRISTMAS BLITZ

CHAPTER ONE

BLITZED

I hit send on my cell phone and shot a text to Nicolas letting him know I'll meet soon. Looks like I'm off to meet some guy whose intensions I can only predict. I press the gas pedal of my beat-up Honda. How could she stick me with the Lakeside Mansion, a.k.a. Hilldale's tour house? I mean, everyone who asks to see it has no intention of ever buying it. Who could blame them? A million and a half dollars is hard to come by in this one-horse town.

Punching Angie Johnson in the face should be legal in all fifty states. I've pictured it in my mind a million times. Her flawless designer mascara runs down her cheeks to her vindictive, deceitful mouth. For once, that smug look disappears from her face. No jury in the world would convict me, especially if they've met my overbearing boss. If only I could afford to quit. Guess I have to put up with her snide comments until I get back on my feet. Her voice echoes in my head. *Holly, you should be happy. If you have the skills, you'll make the sale.* The memory of her crimson hair flying over her shoulder, her words dripping with sarcasm, play over and over again in my mind like a broken record. She pretty much forced me to relist the property if I want to keep my job. Now I have to deal with the ten phone calls a day from the owners asking for updates and she still gets a 50% split on commission if by some miracle it does sell. I guess I have to give her credit. She covers all her bases.

Didn't Angie get her rocks off torturing me, and countless others, all through high school? Sad, if you ask me. Twenty-three years old and owner of Trust Realty but still acting like a prom queen. The car skids on a patch of ice, fishtailing along the winding road. I hold my breath and pump the brake. *Please don't let me crash.* My insurance would skyrocket. The tires grip a few pieces of exposed blacktop, allowing me to regain control. I slump back in the seat and loosen the death grip on my steering wheel. Doesn't matter about Angie, I need this job if I ever want to save up enough to leave Hilldale, Vermont far behind me.

I reach over and turn on the radio. Some music may calm my nerves.

"Hilldale's own NFL football hero, Nick Shaw of the Iowa Talons, will be lighting this year's Christmas tree at the public library's charity event. Be sure to meet and greet our hometown hero this Saturday at Market Square." The announcer's voice, giddy like a schoolgirl's.

I click off the radio and press my head into the headrest. Great, must be nice to be Hilldale royalty. Guess the town plans on bending over backward for Nick to grace us with his presence. I'm sure Angie, his ex, will be on cloud nine. I tap my fingernails on the steering wheel. Well, he does have talent, but when you're born with a silver spoon in your mouth, you get the best training and coaches. Believe me, if I make it out of here, I'll never come back. Nothing here for me but tarnished memories.

I slowly exhale, letting the tension leave my muscles. I've got to think positive. Maybe I can talk this client into looking at a more affordable house, maybe even make a sale. I turn onto the mile-long stretch of private drive, lined with evergreen trees glistening with fresh-fallen snow. Everything is quiet, serene.

Like a scene from an old-time Christmas movie, a complete winter wonderland.

I pull around the cobblestone driveway, circling a three-tiered concrete fountain, and park near the front of the house. No other vehicles are here. Guess I'm a little early. No problem, gives me a few more minutes to prepare my pitch. I glance into the rearview mirror and adjust a few strands of my long blonde hair. Good enough. Okay, first I'll head inside and turn on the fireplace for some ambience, then I'll point out the features of this magnificent property. I rub my hands down my gray skirt, grab the paperwork, and hop out of my car, making my way up the three steps to the huge wooden door.

"The view is amazing," a voice calls out.

I jump back, the tip of my heel sliding on a small patch of ice on the top step. The spec sheets fly through the air, my hands desperately try to grab onto something… anything. I close my eyes tight and brace myself for the blow. A split second later I'm surrounded by muscular arms. I slowly open my eyelids. Light brown eyes meet mine, a unique color like melted caramel, and just as warm.

"You okay? Trust Realty really does bend over backward for their clients." He winks, flashing a smile. Small dimples form, accentuating his chiseled jawline.

Yeah, more like I'm falling apart. I nod. For some reason my mouth refuses to form words. My first week on the job and I've already embarrassed myself. He tips me forward to a standing position and takes a few steps back, limping. This can't be happening. Did I seriously just injure a client? Way to act professional.

I turn toward him and put my hand on his shoulder. "I'm so sorry." I stare down at his leg. Not sure why, it's not like I have X-ray vision or can assess the damage.

He shakes his head. "Nah. Pulled a hamstring last week, no biggie." He slides his hand into his pocket.

I raise my eyes and sweep them across his thick brown hair, illuminated by the rays of sun peeking out from between the clouds. His face, it's... familiar. Have we met? I gasp, louder than expected. Oh my God, why did it take me this long to realize it? It's been five years, not an eternity, and that's not an easily forgettable face.

I hold out my hand, trying to prevent it from trembling. "Holly Clifford, your Trust Realty Agent."

"Nick Shaw." He slides his hand out of his pocket and shakes mine. "Gorgeous."

I quickly pull my hand away. Ah, he's a sweet talker. If he thinks I'm doing anything "off the books" just because he's a famous athlete, he's sadly mistaken. What am I thinking? All of a sudden I decide he's vowing to have his way with me. I must be temporarily insane. I follow his eyes and turn around. Oh, he means the house. Of course he does.

"Would you like to see more?" Heat spreads across my face like wildfire. Why does that sound like a proposition? Maybe I'm better off keeping my mouth shut or reading directly from the spec sheets. Dammit, the spec sheets. I quickly grab four sheets of paper scattered across the drive way and chase the last piece, which is now floating away from a mild gust of wind. I reach out, got it. I shuffle the papers and hand him one of my brand-new business cards. "Follow me."

I navigate around the small ice patch and unlock the door, stepping into a marble foyer. The tiles stretch across the length of the first floor and lead to a great room, with a stone fireplace. A state-of-the-art kitchen with granite countertops and stainless-steel appliances sits behind the great room, along with an eating area and sliding doors that lead right to the lakefront. A double-arched wooden stairway that seems to reach the heavens opens to an enormous landing and hallways on both sides. Wall-to-wall windows grace the back wall of both floors. Last time I took in a view quite like this was when we took our senior

. . .

trip to Killington. Actually, this is better because we're on a private lake.

"Notice the modern architecture with old-world charm." I wave my hand through the air, dropping another spec sheet. I sigh and bend down to pick it up, but Nick grabs it before it hits the ground.

"Let me guess, new to the real estate business?" He hands me the paper, eyeing me suspiciously. "Wait, do we know each other?"

I take the sheet and shove it with the others. He can't possibly remember me from high school. I mean, it's not humanly possible to forget *him*. We had one class together and he sat in the row next to mine and two seats in front. Funny, I can't remember which class but I won't forget the way his bicep flexed every time he nibbled on his pen cap. But there's nothing memorable about me. We never even talked, not once. Plus, I left that nerdy persona behind me. I'm barely recognizable from my senior pictures. Nope. I must remind him of someone else. "Hilldale High?" It's all I can get out. What a stupid question. Like anyone here in town doesn't know he led our team to three district titles.

"Yeah." He rubs his chin. "Mr. Horton's economics class." He drops his hand and flashes that smile. "Your hair was darker and you had glasses but I remember. You sat behind me."

Ah, economics. In light of my current financial situation, that explains a lot. Maybe he's the reason it was the only C on my report card, ever. "Oh, yeah. You're right." I nibble my fingernails.

"Are you a partner in Trust Realty? You went to Columbia, right? I remember, we were the only two people to get into Ivy League schools."

Of course he would remember that. It's not like I regret dropping out not really. I'd do anything for my mother. I'd never leave her and take off when she needed me. Cancer is an evil entity. It sucked the life out of the both of us. Now I'm stuck here until I can dig myself out of this pile of medical bill debt. No matter, if I had the choice again, I'd do it all over. I spent every possible second with my mother and made her life the best I could, just like she always did for me. There's no way I'm telling him my sob story, although he may buy the house out of pity. I mean, he's probably the only person in town who can actually afford it. "Columbia didn't work out."

"That's too bad. But on the plus, you get to stay here."

Why is he saying that like it's a good thing? "For now anyway." I leaf through the papers and pull out the main spec sheet. "The house sits on two acres of lakefront property and includes the boathouse, barbecue, and pier."

He walks forward and looks out onto the lake. "It's amazing. I wish Hilldale had a pro team, I'd stay here forever."

"Really?" I lower my eyebrows and join him, taking in the pristine view.

"Yeah, small towns offer some things that big cities can't. Plus there's no place like home. That's why I'm looking for a place here. For the off-season."

"Is the season over now?" If he starts with the football talk he might as well speak like Charlie Brown's teacher. I'd understand them both about the same.

He nods. "It is for me, pulled my hamstring in the game last week so I'm out for two more games. Since we have no hope for the playoffs, that's the rest of the season."

Could be worse, at least it's not a career-ending injury or anything like that. But he wants to buy a place here. Oh my God, I might actually make a sale today. "I can show you some other properties if you want to see what's on the market."

He walks forward and reaches for the spec sheet. His calloused fingers brush mine, sending tingles through my body. "I doubt anything's better than this."

No building in town captivates you like this one, not even the bed-and-breakfasts along the lake. The most similar is the ski resort the next town over. Maybe he just wanted to take a look at the property for nostalgic reasons.

I hold out my hand. "It was nice to meet you, I mean see you again."

"Yeah, you too." He takes my hand and shakes, not letting go.

"Did you want to see the bedrooms before we go?" Oh my God. Now that definitely sounds like a proposition. The blood drains from my face. "I mean do you want to see the rest of the property?" I yank my hand away.

Is there a job where I could just embarrass myself and get paid for it? Maybe a clown. I'd be the best in the nation. Once he runs into Angie, which I'm sure will happen sooner or later, she'll probably fire me for acting so unprofessional.

"Let's go upstairs." He places his hand in the small of my back and guides me up the steps.

Oh no, he did get the wrong idea. Hate to break it him, but I'm not one of his adoring groupies, or whatever you call them. I'm all business. I step to the side, causing his hand to slide. It slips along my ass on its way down. Why am I so awkward? Seriously, with the way I'm acting, the only way I could be more forward is if I ripped my clothes off.

I swing open the door and let out a slight gasp. The sun shines through the wall-to-wall windows, casting golden rays on the cherry hardwood. I take a few steps forward and gaze out onto the glistening frozen lake, shining like a million diamonds are scattered across the water. Beautiful, like I'm in the Garden of Eden in winter.

"Like what you see?" Nick leans against the doorway, staring forward.

More than I should, and I don't mean just the lake. "It's a beautiful property." I grip the paperwork close to my chest. If I drop it one more time, he's going to think I have some kind of condition. Why the hell am I acting like such a klutz? For God's sake, I was the Sugar Plum Fairy at my church's production of the Nutcracker, not one mistake. Okay, so it was fifteen years ago, but I'd like to think I'm still as coordinated Does Nick Shaw give off an essence that turns women into a ball of nerves?

He walks toward me. "I'd never grow sick of looking at this view every morning." He stops at the window.

Is he referring to the picturesque lake or something else? My heart skips a beat. My God, it's like aliens removed my brain and I'm regressing back to high school, hoping to grab the attention of the hot football star. God, why won't my body get in tune with my brain? Nick could have anyone, in fact he probably already has a girlfriend or wife. I glance at his finger—okay, no wife. Doesn't matter, I have to resist his charm. Not that he showed any interest in me whatsoever. Yep, every innuendo was made by me. Come on, Holly, get it together.

"Yes, the view is breathtaking." I inadvertently nibble at my lip. "Would you like to see more? Of the house? More great views." Oh God, now I'm babbling. "The main bathroom is through those French doors."

He flashes a sexy smile. "Lead the way, Holly." He gestures with his hand.

Just the way he says my name, it sounds so... inviting. I imagined him saying it a million times in my daydreams years ago. The concoction I created wasn't close to as good as reality. Flutters erupt in my stomach. I stand tall, maintaining whatever professionalism I have left.

We walk into the bathroom. "Granite countertops, whirlpool tub overlooking the lake, tile shower with state-of-the art massaging jets, all the bells and whistles." I stand against the counter.

He leans over the tub, taking in the view one more time. The muscles in his shoulders move, causing ripples to form on his black leather jacket.

"Down the hallway to the right are four more bedrooms and

two guest baths." I turn to walk out the door just as he swings around. I slam into his chest. My God, it's like hitting a brick wall. I look down at the floor, afraid to raise my eyes. My face must be a hundred shades of crimson.

"My fault." He lifts my chin, rubbing his thumb along it.

I tip my head up and part my lips, lost for a minute. The house has got nothing on this view. Reality hits me like a freight train. I jerk backward and clear my throat. "Right this way." I hightail it down the hallway.

Nick almost jogs to keep up with me, slightly limping. "You're fast, maybe you should try out for the team."

I stop and turn back toward him. "Sorry." I nibble at my fingernails.

He winks. "Joking."

I drop my hand and nod, letting out the breath I was holding.

He pulls open the door to our right. "How long have you been into real estate?" He walks into the guest bedroom.

"Not long." Great, I'm losing my first potential client. Other than the double block I showed Wednesday, this is my second property. Guess I can't hide my inexperience. I follow him through the door into the spacious room, fidgeting with my fingers.

"No worries, I'm a rookie too." He travels the length of the room near the window. "Nice, the architect wanted to separate the master suite. Everyone needs privacy."

Makes sense. His life is pretty much public knowledge now that he's hit the big time. Unless he's looking for privacy for other reasons. "Yeah, this place is pretty secluded."

"Sometimes it's good to hide." He raises an eyebrow and continues out of the room and down the hallway.

What's he trying to hide? It's really none of my business anyway. It's not like I'll see him again after today. Except maybe on television if I happen to flip through the channels. I'm dying to know more about him though. He's kind of mysterious and not a shred of the typical meathead jock. Why am I obsessing over this? I clearly need to stop watching Lifetime movies. Maybe if I actually focus on the task at hand, I can show him a house he'll love, make a sale, and decrease some of my debt so I'm closer to getting out of this place.

"Feel free to take a look around. I'll wait downstairs in case you have any questions." I reach for the banister to start down the steps.

Nick grabs my wrist. "Wait."

His touch sends goose bumps across my skin. I freeze like a deer in headlights then turn toward him.

"I was checking out the lakefront before. Are the water levels controlled?"

All the blood drains from my face. A completely legitimate question any Realtor selling a property should know, and I have absolutely no clue. I pull my hand away and leaf through the paperwork. My fingers tremble every time I touch the corner of the page.

He moves behind me and reads the papers over my shoulders. I slump and read as fast as I can, desperately trying to find the answer. No such luck.

Nick moves forward, so he's almost pressing up against me and points to the paper. His arm swings around over mine. "Right here. It says there's a Lake Association that controls the dam to prevent flooding."

I step forward and rub my forehead with my hand. "I'm so sorry. Guess I'm not cut out for the real estate business." I face him and shake my head. "Angie's going to crucify me."

"Angie?" He crinkles his eyebrows. "Angie Johnson?"

"The one and only. She owns Trust Realty now. Her grandfather left it to her in his will."

He chuckles. "Amazing it's still up and running." He steps forward and ducks down so we're eye to eye. "What Angie doesn't know won't hurt her."

I flash a smile. "Do you still keep in touch?" Why would I ask that? It's none of my business.

"Nah. Not since sophomore year of college." He stands and takes a step back. "Hard to stay in touch with everyone."

"Yeah, me neither. I mean, except for the few times I meet up with someone at the store."

"Come on, Rookie." He places his hand in the small of my back, again, and leads me down the steps.

This time I don't pull away, I don't even flinch. I just let him guide me down the stairs. When we make it to the bottom, I reach in my coat for my car keys. "If you're up for it, I can show you some other properties you may be interested in." I pull up the zipper. "Or I can have Angie fill you in on the details of this property if you'd rather deal with her."

"I don't need to see anything else and I don't need Angie." He slides his cell phone out of his jacket pocket.

So he's not interested. No biggie. It's not like I expected the sale anyway. Even though it took years longer than I'd hoped, I met the legendary Nick Shaw. Now I need to stay as far away from him as possible and focus on my goal. Who knows, maybe I'll sell the next property I show. I hold out my hand. "It was nice to meet you. I hope you find what you're looking for."

He takes my hand and holds it tight. "I found exactly what I'm looking for."

Those eyes could pierce an armored tank. Did it just get ten degrees hotter in here? "Huh?" That's all I can manage to say.

"The house. I want to put in an offer."

My jaw drops. Wait, did I hear him right? "You want to buy this property?"

"Yeah." He leans toward the foyer, still holding my hand. "I can probably put a twelve-foot Christmas tree right there, near the fireplace." He points with his free hand.

I nod. "Um, I think you need someone more experienced than

11

me to help you get the best price. Maybe Angie should work with you from here on out."

He drops my hand. "Nope, I want to work with you." He presses a few buttons on his cell phone. "What's your number?"

Wait, I'm not ready for this. Not for any of it. "I really think you need someone else to…"

He holds up a finger. "Never mind, got your card right here."

I lean over and watch him type in the digits under the contact named Rookie. Cute.

"Looks like the rookie made the big sale." He winks. "How long until the paperwork is ready?"

Great, another legitimate question and I'm drawing a blank.. He definitely needs someone more experienced for a sale like this. Why does he insist on working with me? I'm probably the most unprofessional person he's ever encountered. This is a terrible idea. I've got to talk him out of this. I shrug.

"No worries. I'll call you tomorrow. We can talk over lunch."

No way. Everything needs to be done at the office. That way, I'll have access to other Realtors and resources. Absolutely nothing regarding this sale can be done outside of the Trust Realty office. I look up at his strong jawline and continue to his eyes. "Okay." *Dammit.*

CHAPTER TWO

HOLIDAY MAGIC?

A sweet, enchanting scent flows through the air. I pump a few more sprays of Holiday Fantasy onto the thick sample strips. Kransen's Department store is a Christmas wonderland complete with Santa and an array of helpers. I adjust my Santa hat and greet a middle-aged woman wearing a red coat with a candy cane brooch pinned to the lapel.

"Ma'am, have you tried our signature fragrance? It's on sale for the season. Who knows, it may make your holiday wishes come true." I hand her a sample strip.

She holds it to her nose and smiles. "Thank you. I'll give it some thought." She tucks the strip in her pocket and scurries through the aisle.

I never thought holiday wishes did come true, not until I met Nick Shaw. So the paperwork took longer than expected, and lunch didn't work out, but hey, I managed to get him a great deal. Plus, the commission I make will render me almost debt free. No more pushing perfume on every person who walks in here. I feel like a car salesman, trying to show off the features of a fragrance and hoping to seal the deal. I sigh. Lunch would've been nice though.

Another woman shuffles through the aisle. Two coworkers spot her Fendi bag. They both charge toward her, sporting million-dollar smiles and a holding a bottle of perfume in each of their hands. What's worse, competing for customers or hassling them for a sale? I won't miss a thing about this job. But maybe I'll wait until after the New Year to give my two weeks' notice. It wouldn't hurt to make a few extra dollars.

I set my perfume bottle on the counter and lean against the glass case. If I can fill out my college applications by the end of February, I have a shot at getting into a fall program... somewhere. Nothing ventured, nothing gained. I've got to at least try. Who knows, law school might even pan out.

"Good afternoon, Holly." The department manager, Debbie, gives the perfume cases a quick look over.

I stand up tall and quickly grab my sample bottle. "We're pretty

busy today." Great, I slack off for a split second and I get caught. Typical.

She nods and scurries around the department, making sure everything is in order.

A few customers window shop the glass cases. I gaze out into the main aisle. Santa Claus is the belle of the ball. The line wraps around almost to the toy department. Probably a marketing strategy. Nonetheless, every child's face lights up when Santa lets out the ole ho, ho, ho. Complete magic. If only that magic existed for adults.

Giggles and loud whispers fill the perfume counter. What the hell is going on? My colleagues have turned into teenagers. Are they plotting some devious plan to win the Kransen's Christmas contest for the most sales?

I lean toward the end of the counter, trying to listen. "Rich *and* gorgeous. What are the chances of a guy like that showing up here?" Janice tucks her long brown hair behind her ear.

"About one in a hundred million." Rita laughs, playfully nudging Janice.

Apparently Jon Bon Jovi just walked in and I've missed it. I peek around two customers to get a glimpse of this so-called man candy. I gasp and take a step back. Oh my God. He's here? I rub my eyes and glance again. Yep, it's Nick. I can't let him see me here. What am I supposed to say... something like "Hey, Nick, you just bought a seven-figure house from the perfume girl"?

Maybe Debbie will let me take my break now. I search the main aisle and perfume department. *Dammit*, she's nowhere to be found. Okay, no problem. I'll just blend in and he'll pass me right by. What's the chance he's buying perfume anyway?

I take a few steps to the side and stand tall behind the mirrored pillar. I look down and chuckle to myself. Well, this day certainly took an interesting turn. Hiding from a guy who changed my life for the better. Bet I'll be talking about this on the couch of a psychiatrist's office someday.

"Hello, sir, can I interest you in a sample?" Janice's voice is as fake as a three-dollar bill. I can just imagine how low she managed to get that V-neck to plunge. Guess she's looking for husband number four. Not something I'd be proud of at twenty-eight, but she seems to deal with it just fine.

A gray-haired woman clutching an overfilled shopping bag walks toward me. She drops the bag at my feet. "Ma'am, is that a new fragrance?"

I look down at the glass bottle encrusted with silver gems. "Oh, yes." I search my pocket for a sample strip.

"No worries." She holds out her wrist.

I spray some on her wrist. There's no way he'll recognize my voice. Not after our brief conversation. What am I thinking? He's probably gone anyway.

She smiles. "Very nice. I think I'd like a bottle."

"Of course." Awesome, first sale of the day. "Right this way." I navigate around the pillar and step up to my counter.

"Holly?"

Dammit. I close my eyes for a split second and gather my thoughts. Guess it's not possible to die from embarrassment or I'd be six feet under by now. I spin around. "Hi."

He scrunches his eyebrows. "You work here too?"

Oh boy. "Yeah, great discounts on merchandise." Seriously? That's the best I could come up with? Guess my brain is fried. Or Nick manages to turn it completely off.

"Nice. I'll have to remember that."

Janice steps in front of me. "You know, we've got some great deals on men's and women's fragrances. Which are you in the market for?" She runs her tongue along her lips. Real subtle.

I turn my attention toward the gray-haired woman and ring up her purchase. "Thank you and Merry Christmas."

"Merry Christmas, dear." She hoists up her bag and heads out of the store.

"Maybe both." Nick glances at the perfume case. "What's your favorite, Holly?"

"For whom? I mean, men's or women's?" Heat spreads across my cheeks like wildfire.

"Something for my mom."

I grab the bottle closest to me. Perfect. Winter's Frost. "This one's my favorite." I spray a sample strip and wave it a few times.

He steps forward and takes hold of my hand. His calloused fingers glide along my skin, sending chills shooting through me. I breathe slowly, trying to calm my nerves. He lifts my hand to his face.

"She'll love it. I'll take two." He smiles, slowly releasing my hand.

"Two?" I reach in my pocket for the key to the case.

He rubs the back of his neck. "Yeah, my sister won't let me

live it down if she likes Mom's present more than hers." He chuckles. "Now everyone's happy."

"Anyone else you need something for, hon?" Janice chimes in. "Kransen's is having a big contest for its sales associates."

Nick rubs his chin. "What kind of contest?"

Janice waves her arm. "Oh, we're trying for the grand prize. The associate with the most sales by close on Christmas Eve night wins a one-thousand-dollar bonus."

"Interesting." He nods.

Janice turns toward a couple perusing the far glass case. "Duty calls." She trots over to the potential customers.

"Looks like you've got some competition." Nick peruses the row of perfume samples.

What's that supposed to mean? I'm not the competitive type. Probably why I'm in last place for this contest. "Who? Janice?" I shake my head. "She comes on so strong, she usually scares people away." *There's your warning.*

We turn toward her just as she's walking behind the couple, moving faster by the second.

Nick chuckles. "Point taken." He picks up a bottle then sets it back down on the counter. "Where else am I going to find you?"

Other than lying on my couch, nowhere special. "Two jobs is my limit." I straighten the bottles into a perfect line and move behind the counter to ring up Nick's purchase.

He leans against the counter. "How about for fun? Is Josie's Café still the happening bar on Saturday nights?"

I nod. "The one and only."

"What time do you get off?"

Wait. Is he asking me out? My hands turn to jelly. In a split second the perfume bottle slides from my fingers. Nick reaches down over the counter with catlike reflexes and catches it before it hits the floor.

I gasp. "Thank you."

He sets the bottle on the counter and gives me a quick salute. "At your service."

I laugh. Wow, first time in a while. It's like he's my guardian angel. *Please don't let me wake up if this is all a dream.* What am I thinking? He probably swoons someone in every town he stops in. Not sure why I'm the lucky one here in Hilldale. Sure, I wished for it years ago, but that was another lifetime. I've got to get over this ridiculous crush. For God's sake, high school was an eternity ago and I'm a grown woman. Rich, handsome athletes don't just storm into town and rescue the damsel in distress. Unfortunately, life isn't a fairy tale.

"Did you want anything else?" I ring his purchase into the register.

"Maybe." He looks down into the glass case then back up at me. "You never answered my question."

"About the perfume?" I place the bottle in the bag. "What did you want to know?"

He stands up and presses his palms against the glass. "Want to go to Josie's after work? It's been a while. I could use a tour guide."

Oh God. I can't go there. Besides the fact I pretty much avoided all of Josie's dinner invites, it's like a high school reunion of everyone who couldn't get out of this town. Plus, if I walked into somewhere like that with Nick Shaw, I'd be tossed like a dirty penny. No thanks, I played the wallflower my whole life. No need to revisit those days. Besides, he knows half the town, and the other half is dying to meet him. I'd just get in his way and I certainly don't want to make my life any more complicated, especially now that I can see the light at the end of the tunnel. Surprise visits from hometown heroes who want to hang out with me is not in the master plan.

"I work until close and the town hasn't changed in eons. Plus, it's not my scene."

He scrunches his eyebrows. "What is your scene?"

I shrug. "I usually just hang out at home with Jack." Not like I can afford to blow money on drinks and dinner. A quiet night at home is more my style.

He bites his lip. "Have I met Jack?"

Not yet. Best man in my life at the moment, though. I muffle a smile. "Nah, he keeps to himself. A real homebody. Loves to cuddle. He's probably staring out the window right now waiting for me."

He flashes a smile. "Does Jack happen to purr?"

I chuckle. "Like a champ." I slide the bag toward him. "I found him outside last winter curled up underneath my deck. He was freezing. Once I looked into those sad, green eyes, I was hooked. Named him Jack after Jack Frost. Now he's spoiled just like every cat should be." Great. I'm babbling again.

"He seems like a standup guy. I'd love to meet him sometime."

I smile. I'd rather go to Josie's and take my chances with the over-enthused townsfolk than let Nick see where I live. The Realtor who lives in the crappiest house in town. The house needs some serious repairs. If I can sell it and break close to even, I'll call it a win. "That'll be $82.75."

He slides a hand from the counter to his pockets. "I'm still shopping." He walks the length of the counter then strolls back toward me. I focus on the curves of his muscular legs, dancing against the thick, dark denim. "I need more gifts."

What's he up to? "Okay, what can I get for you?" I fidget with my fingers.

"I'm a last-minute shopper." He taps his lip. "I'll need something for my sister-in-law, my aunt, my nieces, my godchild, my offensive team, their wives, Coach, Coach's wife, and my brother."

I hold up my hands. "Sorry, all I can suggest is perfume and cologne. I think you might need Santa himself to help you."

"Great idea."

I smirk. "Believe me, if I knew Santa, I wouldn't have two jobs."

"I meant the perfume." He looks directly at me, his eyes intense. "You shouldn't work so hard."

Like I have a choice. "You want more perfume?"

He nods. "Yep. I'll need about 40 bottles of cologne and 50 bottles of perfume. Whatever fragrances you think." He winks.

What? Am I in *The Twilight Zone*? "You're joking, right?"

"Hell, no. This is great. One stop and I'm finished Christmas shopping." He slaps his credit card on the counter.

Oh my God. He's really buying just about every bottle in my case. Did the fumes infiltrate his brain? Maybe he's had a bad reaction to these samples. Does he even know what he's doing? "Are you sure?"

"Yes. Please ring me up, miss" He flashes a sexy smile.

I bend down and grab four large shopping bags. Let's see, I'll mix it up a bit to give him a variety. I unlock the cases and peruse the stock. Looks like I'll have enough to fill this enormous order. Christmas at Nick's must be amazing. If all the players exchange presents, I can see why he needs the Lakeside Mansion. The gifts will just about fit under the tree in that great room. Not that presents make a difference. It's all about spending time with your loved ones. If I could skip to January, I'd do it in a heartbeat. Holidays aren't the same when you're alone. At least Jack loves my roasted turkey. I ring up each bottle and then place it in a shopping bag, paying careful attention to be sure the bags hold the weight. I place the last one in a bag and look up at the register.

I blink a few times then focus on the green letters lighting up the screen of the register. Oh God, there's no way he expected it to be so expensive. I swallow hard and turn toward Nick. "It comes to $4500.00." I bite my lip.

He slides the credit card across the counter. "Do you take Visa?"

I nod and take the credit card with my trembling hand, quickly sliding it through the register. The receipt begins to print. A plethora of paper spews out, rolling down onto the floor. Janice glares over from the main aisle. She adjusts her glasses, squinting. Eyes burn through me. All I can do is stare at the paper turning into a pile on the floor. Maybe Kransen's should think about going green.

Janice struts over, her heels click against the tiles. "Is something wrong with your register?" She joins me behind the counter. "Want help?"

I take a step back and shake my head.

She picks up the receipt and reads through the list of items. "Holly, did your button stick?" She looks over at me, then at the four bags in front of Nick.

I take the receipt from her hand. "Nope, we're good here. I'm just ringing up the purchase." Finally, the register stops printing. I rip off the receipt and toss it into the bag.

Janice's eyes widen like flying saucers. "You bought all of these?" She looks down at my empty perfume case.

"Just about finished shopping now." He holds out his hand and takes his credit card.

Janice pats my shoulder before walking away. "Looks like the contest is over," she whispers in my ear.

How could I be so blind? Of course Nick did this to make sure I won the contest. But why? If he thinks I'm his next charity case, he's sadly mistaken. I can take care of myself and don't need to be dazzled by his money and status. I tap my fingers on the counter.

"Something wrong?" he asks.

"I just realized with your sale, I've got this contest in the bag."

He crinkles his forehead. "Isn't that good?"

I shrug. "What do you think you're doing?"

"Christmas shopping." He slides his credit card back into his wallet and sticks it in his back pocket. "Spreading a little holiday cheer."

I fold my arms over my chest. "You're in luck. There are at least five festivals this week. You can spread all kinds of cheer."

He leans his elbow on the counter. His bicep flexes, pushing against the tight leather of his jacket. "That reminds me... never mind."

I drop my arms and take a step forward. "What?"

"Do you like books?"

Um, I read at least three of them a week. Sometimes more. "Sure."

Janice wipes down the top of the counter behind us, pretending not to listen.

"There's this charity event for the children's library on Saturday. I'm the guest referee." He stands up and runs a hand through his hair. "Angie's bragging all over town about selling the Lakeside Mansion. I thought the real girl who sealed the deal might want to come with me?"

What a bitch. It's just like Angie to go around taking credit that doesn't belong to her. I grimace. I'm not all that enthused to join in on social events, even though years ago I would have cut off my right arm to go to one with Nick. I can picture it now. The judging eyes, the whispers, the talk about how I gave up my life to take care of my mom and how I'm destined to become an old maid. Ugh, I don't know about this.

He gathers up his bags. "That is, if Jack approves."

Janet drops her paper towel and holds her hands up. She mouths the word *yes*.

My lips upturn to a smile. Ah, what the hell. "I think I can talk him into it." This isn't a date. Just two friends hanging out together, that's all. Even though we never were really friends, nor did we hang out. No way is he picking me up. "I'll meet you there."

"You sure? I can swing by and get you."

"No," I say, much louder than I planned. "I'll meet you there after work. What time does it start?"

He takes his keys out of a pocket. "Two o'clock. See you Saturday."

"Wait, I'm not going to get tackled or anything, right?"

He shrugs. "No promises." He winks and heads out of the store.

An inferno engulfs my face. It happened. Five years later than I'd hoped, but Nick Shaw actually asked me out. Better late than never, I guess.

CHAPTER THREE

JOINING THE CROWD

Why does time change everything? Five years ago everyone who walked past would stop and congratulate me on my scholarship or ask about my mom or at least acknowledge that I exist. Not anymore. I hang my head low and trudge forward toward the makeshift football field at Hilldale Park. Dozens of people scurry past me, blending into the crowd. Last time I saw this many people in one place was when Billy Joel played a concert up north. Then again, Nick Shaw is pretty much a rock star in this town.

Snow crunches under my boots, and a light breeze blows a few stray snow flurries across my cheeks. Why did I let Nick buy all that perfume? It was clearly a mercy purchase. It's like he thinks I'm some charity case that he has to save, a poor soul he pities. Sure, I'm not in the best place right now, but I can take care of myself. If my brain would just catch up with my mouth, I could've told him thanks but no thanks. Just like I should've when I agreed to come here. I guess I'm obligated to after all he's done for me. This is it. My mind's made up. After today, we only talk on a business basis.

"Hey, Rookie."

I lift my head and an involuntary smile graces my face. Nick waves his arm like he's about to land a plane. The black-and-white referee shirt accentuates every curve. Yeah, not sure I'm up for the challenge of getting through today.

I wave back and walk onto the field. Eyes burn through me like a spotlight follows my every move. Maybe being invisible is better. I gaze out onto the sidelines filled with young boys, maybe about eight years old, half of them dressed in red jerseys and the other half dressed in green. Their rosy cheeks almost as bright as their smiles. Nick gestures for me to join him.

Wait, aren't I here for moral support? I'm certainly not part of the event. I point toward myself and mouth the word *me*.

He nods and mouths the word *yeah*.

Oh boy. What the hell have I gotten myself into? I know about as much about football as I do about rocket science, maybe less. I oblige and meet him in the middle of the field. Everyone watches as though wondering why in God's name I'm out here. Actually, I'm wondering

the same thing.

"Okay, Rookie. Here's your whistle." He places a candy cane–colored whistle tied to a red string around my neck.

I shake my head. "No way. I can't referee."

"Sure you can." He adjusts his hat and glances at his watch.

I grab his arm, holding tighter than necessary. It barely gets around his rock-hard bicep. Wait, what did I want to tell him? I pull my mind back into reality and slowly release my grip. "I'm sorry, I don't know the rules."

"Good thing you've got a great teacher." He picks up the whistle attached to my neck and blows.

My heart pounds against my chest. There's no way I'm making it through this day unscathed.

He slides his arm around my waist, guiding me forward.

"When I throw one of these yellow flags, you blow the whistle." He pulls a yellow flag from his pocket.

Seems simple enough. I guess I'll just have to keep my eyes on Nick the whole time. I mean, it *is* for charity. It's almost like it's my public duty to do so.

He slides his hand down, grazing my skin on the way. A chill, not at all related to the weather, flows through me. Okay, time to focus.

Nick gestures for the kids to make their way to the field. A herd of them run toward us. I plant my feet firmly on the ground and my eyes on Nick. A few thick strands peek out from underneath his cap, moving in the light breeze.

"Holly."

I jump and hold the whistle to my lips.

He shakes his head. "Time for the coin toss. You call it." He tosses an oversized coin into the air.

It lands on the hard grass. Looks like it's... Santa? Is that supposed to be heads or tails? I bite my lip and raise my head. "Santa?" I shrug.

The kids in the red jerseys cheer. I snatch the coin and flip it over. Ah, elves must be the green team.

Nick jogs to the sideline, the muscles in his legs bulging against those dark jeans with every move. I fixate on every inch of his body. God, what's wrong with me? Of course he's in tip-top shape, he's a professional athlete. So he's hot, and I mean carved-from-a-block-of-marble kind of hot. Doesn't matter, this silly infatuation ends today. In fact, once I get home I'm pouring a glass of wine and filling out my first application—University of Virginia. First requirement is to get out of this town, preferably somewhere warmer.

Nick returns with a football and hands it to a little brown-haired boy with rosy cheeks. "Ready?"

The boy nods.

Nick points toward me.

What does he want me to do now? Oh right, the whistle. I blow the whistle and follow Nick to the sidelines. If all games were this cute, I might actually watch football. The kids run up and down the field, trying their best to catch the ball. Some succeed, some don't, but none of it matters. No one is keeping score, this is purely for fun. Wish I could say that about more things in life.

Nick glances at his watch and points to me. I grab the candy cane whistle and blow.

"Half-time," he shouts.

I rub my hands together, trying to create some warmth. Even though it's forty degrees today, the crisp winter air has turned me into a Popsicle.

He takes my hand and brings it to his mouth, slowly breathing warm air on my skin. It melts my soul. He lifts his head. "Ready for a hot chocolate?"

I nod, even though I don't want to move a muscle. Our eyes lock and a magnetizing energy refuses to let either of us break from the trance. Hot chocolate has nothing on Nick Shaw.

"You two know each other... outside of business?" Angie flashes her famous degrading stare.

She must've practiced that horrid look in the mirror for years to fine-tune it so well. I've seen it tear people's emotions to shreds. One glance and I'm back to that invisible wallflower, just an outcast who has no business being part of this event, especially with Nick.

Nick drops my hand. Great, guess she turned him into the popular jock that can't be seen with the likes of me. It's like I've regressed ten years in the last ten seconds. Doesn't matter anyway, I'll be long gone soon and I plan to leave all the tainted memories here.

"Guess I can't seem to stay away from her." He shifts his focus from Angie back to me, instantly trapping us in the force field.

. . .

"Wow, you have changed." She taps her high-heeled boots on the hard field.

"You haven't changed a bit." He faces her as if he's protecting me from a mass murderer.

She giggles and tosses her hair over a shoulder. Of course she'd think it's a compliment. In her eyes, no one would ever insult the queen of Hilldale. Nevertheless, I can't help but feel confident. Like whatever she says or does makes no difference. She's lost all the power she once held over all of us.

Nick places his hand in the small of my back. The soft touch sends a kaleidoscope of butterflies fluttering through my stomach. No one's ever had this effect on me before. Not even when I finally lost my virginity to Billy Jones in the backseat of his mother's Camry. Yet Nick can drive my body wild in the middle of a public place with one sweep of his hand? I'm in so much trouble, more than I ever thought possible.

"Catch you later, Angie. Got to grab a quick hot chocolate before duty calls." He guides me forward, leaving Angie alone on the field.

I muffle a smirk. Even though I'm dying to turn and see the look on her face, I walk ahead with my head held a little higher than usual. She'll never get the best of me again.

A woman greets us at the hot chocolate counter. She's young, maybe eighteen at most, and flashes a smile that could light up the tallest Christmas tree. I'm sure it's directed at Nick.

We each take a cup of hot chocolate. She nuzzles into Nick, pulling him into a hug. The hot chocolate sloshes to the top of the cup, almost pouring over the side. Guess he's into younger women, just like most professional athletes. Why is it that guys want younger women? It can't be purely based on looks. No one is that shallow. I've got to say, up to this point he had me fooled. Maybe acting is his true calling.

"Meet my rookie referee, Holly." He gestures toward me.

The woman holds her hand out to me. "Hey, I'm Gina. Nick's favorite sister." She snickers.

"Yeah, also my only sister." He gives her a quick squeeze. "Catch ya at the tree lighting ceremony later."

She waves and trots over to the concession counter.

Alright, so maybe I jumped the gun by stereotyping Nick into the rich playboy. It's just that on one hand he acts like he can buy anything, including affection. Hence the whole perfume stunt he pulled. Still can't figure out the motive behind that one. Then on the other hand he's a sweet, all-American hometown hero, trying to use his success to help the town. They're two opposite ends of the spectrum. So which one is the real Nick?

He nudges my shoulder. "Plan on watching them fire up that Douglas fir after this? Egg nog's on me."

No way. After this game is over, I consider my obligation fulfilled. I shake my head. "I'm heading home after the game. Lots to catch up on." *Please don't let him ask me to elaborate.* Curling up with Jack and one of my book boyfriends is my plan for the evening.

Two men dressed in black tailored suits approach. Wait, that's Mayor Whitman. I pat down my shirt, adjusting the hem to eliminate any wrinkles. What am I doing? It's not like I'm in the presence of the president.

"Nick, you're a generous man." He shakes Nick's hand. "This is Mr. Green from the library."

"Pleased to meet you." Mr. Green shakes Nick's hand and tips his hat toward me.

My lips upturn to a smile. Never had a hat tipped at me before, it's like I'm on a modern version of *Little House on the Prairie.*

Nick nods. "Thank you, sir. I'm happy to help out such a great cause."

Everything about him sucks the rational thought from my body. He's so damn appealing, from his chiseled jaw and perfect body to his willingness to help out whomever he can. God, he's the whole package. I guess guys like him do exist, unless he's the only one. I always thought I'd have a better chance of meeting Santa Claus than a guy like Nick.

"Can we get a picture for the Sunday paper?" The mayor stands next to Nick and gestures for a man with a camera, probably a reporter.

I take a few steps to the side, trying to give them the necessary space.

"Sure thing." Nick hooks his arm around my waist and pulls me toward him, refusing to let go.

I try to pull away but he tightens his grip. The camera man scoots down in front of us. Why on earth is he forcing me to be in this picture? I've given nothing other than a few hours of my time. I certainly don't deserve to be in the paper.

Nick releases his grip but keeps an arm loosely around my waist. His strong fingers exert just enough pressure on my skin to make my body involuntarily move toward him. I want to get as far away from him possible but don't want to move a muscle, like a catch-22.

The mayor steps forward. "Thanks, Nick. Hope you and your little lady are coming to the tree lighting ceremony tonight." He holds up his pointer finger and flashes an expression like a lightbulb just lit up in his brain. "Why don't you two lead the countdown and flip the switch to light up the tree?" He sports an ear-to-ear grin.

"What do you say, Rookie?" Nick slowly slides his arm down.

Is there some sort of mind-altering substance in the hot chocolate? Hell no. There's no way I'm taking part in anything with him other than signing the documents to close on the mansion. Today I've participated in more than I have in the last four years. I'm at my limit. I turn toward Nick, about to tell him no, and focus on the caramel puppy dog eyes grazing the sexier-

than-sin chiseled face. My mind shuts down completely. "Okay."
Dammit.

"Don't look at me like that. I'll be home in forty-five minutes, one
hour tops."

Jack sits tall on my kitchen counter, piercing me with those
green eyes, and then turns his focus to licking the dark gray fur
of his paw. He knows exactly what's going on. It's like he's saying,
"Yeah, okay. You're going to just ditch Nick and take off. Sure
you are."

I've got to stop getting myself into these situations with Nick.
I don't even know how the hell it keeps happening. We've been in
each other's company long enough that I should be immune to
his hotness factor. If he weren't so damn charming, maybe I'd be
able to think long enough to make an actual decision. Amazing,
my brain just shuts itself right down like Nick has some type of
mind control device. Not anymore. I'm focused, cool, and
collected. I fling my purse over my shoulder and head out the
door. Time to light up this damn tree and get home to start the
rest of my life.

The cool air invigorates my senses. I gaze at the plethora of stars
lighting up the clear night sky. Perfect weather for this event. I
exhale, leaving a stream of vapor floating through the air. Okay,
it's now or never, and apparently never isn't an option I can live
with. I click the key fob, locking my car doors, and march
through the parking lot to the center of town.

Market Square resembles a Norman Rockwell painting. Pine
garland adorned with big red bows drapes across the white

gazebo in the center of the square, and lighted snowflakes glow on every lamppost. At least two hundred people have gathered around, swaying to Christmas music sung by the barbershop quartet. Even Hilldale Bakery set up a small area of cookies and hot cocoa for the crowd. And in the center of the white gazebo stands a Douglas fir, waiting to light up the town. Jeez, if I concocted a perfect Christmas scene in my head, it would look just like this. Nick emerges from the shadows with Mayor Whitman. His body illuminated by the soft glow of the street lamp makes him resemble a golden god. I take that back—this scene is much better than the one in my head.

I slide my hands into my coat pocket and step up onto the sidewalk. Nick spots me instantly. I nibble on my lip. Okay, just light up the tree, maybe gulp down a hot chocolate, and I'm out of here. Nick and I need to have a more professional relationship anyway. Especially since the closing on the Lakeside Mansion is Monday. Such a quick closing is unheard of—amazing what a lot of money can accomplish.

He shakes the mayor's hand and walks toward me. I stand frozen, not from the weather, but from the sexy smile meant for me, gracing the face of most appealing human being I've ever laid eyes upon. Heat floods through my body. Even Frosty didn't melt this fast on a scorching summer day.

"Hey, Rookie, ready to light up the night?"

"I've got to head out right afterward." I cover my mouth with my hand. What the hell is wrong with me? Now my brain decides it's time to dominate. Typical. I drop my hand to my side but my mouth refuses to form any words. Guess my brain decided to shut itself off again.

He rubs his chin. "Do you moonlight as a secret agent?" He chuckles.

"I'd tell you but I'd have to kill you." Best line I can come up with.

"I'll figure out your mystery… sooner or later." He holds out his arm.

I entwine my arm with his and walk along the sidewalk as if we're king and queen of the town. Everyone stares but not in the judging or pitying way I'm used to, they're smiling like they're happy to see us. Well, happy to see Nick anyway. Strange, it's the first time I've actually wanted to be part of a Hilldale event. I'm either rapidly going insane or I'm starting to see this town through Nick's eyes.

Okay, enough of the daydream. Back to the task at hand. "So what's the plan? Do we flip a switch or something?" Nick can probably just stand by the tree, and the energy scorching from his body will cause it to burst into flames.

"I'd tell you but I'd have to kill you." He winks.

"Cute." I smirk.

"Mayor Whitman is going to start a countdown after the barbershop quartet sings "It's the Most Wonderful Time of the Year." Then we both pull down a lever in the gazebo and the lights turn on." He slides his hand down to mine and intertwines our fingers together. "Don't worry, Rookie. I'll show you the ropes."

Yeah, exactly what I'm afraid of. We step up onto the platform of the gazebo along with Mayor Whitman. Everyone turns toward the three of us standing near the evergreen. The music starts as if it's on a timer.

Nick wraps his arm around my waist and slowly sways to the music. I mimic his movements, letting him take control of my body. My heart rate doubles in a matter of seconds. I fidget with my fingers, trying to compose myself.

"Welcome, everyone, to the annual Tree Lighting Ceremony in Market Square." Mayor Whitman breaks my trance.

I take a step to the side, moving just far enough away from Nick to maintain my brain function. Instrumental Christmas music has never been so sexy. How can I let myself turn to mush every time he's near me? It's like he's performing the Jedi mind trick without even trying.

"I'm pleased to announce that Iowa Talons wide receiver, Nick Shaw, has come back to Hilldale to celebrate with us. He and our own Holly Clifford will light up this year's Christmas tree."

Hundreds of cheers fill the space, clapping and waving. I gasp. A tingle sweeps up the back of my neck and spreads to my cheeks like wildfire. I guess the town does remember I exist. Who am I kidding, these cheers are for Nick but for some reason I feel different... accepted. Is it really just because Nick is standing next to me or have I misconceived the way this town thinks of me?

The barbershop quartet begins a medley of Christmas songs. Most of the town joins in and sings along. Even Nick lends his pipes to the cause, and he's a much better singer than I expected. God, it's like he can do anything. Next he'll announce he's single handedly declared world peace.

The familiar verse of "It's The Most Wonderful Time of the Year" resonates through the cool air. Butterflies flutter through my stomach and dryness takes over my mouth. Jeez, why am I getting so worked up over flipping a switch? Not much to mess up, unless I trip and knock over the tree or something crazy like that. I fidget with my fingers. *Please don't let my clumsiness take over and ruin this night.*

Mayor Whitman takes the microphone from its stand and holds it to his mouth. "Ten... nine... eight... seven..."

My breathing increases like I'm about to hyperventilate.

The crowd joins in, "Six... five... four..."

My arms tremble. How silly. It's not like I'm in this alone. Nick won't let anything go wrong. Nothing bad ever happens to him. Maybe he's my good luck charm. Oh God, or I could be his nemesis. I bite at my lip.

Nick slides his fingers along mine and takes my hand. Goose bumps flood over me. My mind goes completely blank. For a split second, the only thing that exists is the two of us. We take a few steps forward toward the lever.

"Ready?" he asks at the same instant he puts our hands on the lever, together.

I nod.

"Three… two… one."

He pulls down, my hand moving in unison with his.

Thousands of colorful lights blaze through the clear night. The crowd hoots and hollers, the men, women, and children of Hilldale cheering at the top of their lungs. I pull away, turning around toward the tree and taking in the magnificent sight. Doubt it's brighter than the smile that is now hurting my cheeks. Last time I sported a grin like this was the Christmas before Mom got sick. She wanted a Vera Bradley purse so bad but knew we couldn't afford it. Every time we passed by them at Kransen's her face lit up for a moment. I saved all my money from my job at Jenna's Ice Cream Parlor and surprised her on Christmas morning. Best Christmas of my life, although tonight's events are coming in at a close second. Who would've thought some holiday cheer would creep back into my life?

The barbershop quartet breaks into "O Christmas Tree."

Nick puts his arm around my waist and sways. He quickly joins in the singing. I mimic his movements and before I know it, I'm singing too. I'm actually singing a Christmas carol in Market Square with Nick Shaw. If someone had told me I'd be here right now, I'd have had them committed. Amazing how things can change in an instant.

Mayor Whitman waits for the song to end then holds up the microphone. "We've got hot cocoa and cookies at Mrs. Claus's corner, and don't forget kids of all ages can see the big guy himself, Santa Claus!" He points toward Santa, sitting in a large chair flanked by two elves passing out candy canes.

"So what do you say? Wanna see the big guy, or are you late to go save the world?" Nick flashes that million-dollar smile. He runs a hand through his hair, creating a sexy mess.

What am I thinking? It's like every time I set a goal for myself, I drop it to hang out with Nick. This has to stop. I said I'd stay an hour and already I'm twenty minutes past due. Of course, on the other hand Nick is here for only a short time. Soon he'll be back to the grind, traveling with the Talons. Would it be so bad to spend a little time with him while he's in town? I mean, it's not like I'll see him after that. He'll be traveling and I'll be long gone. Can't hurt to spend a little time together, right? Jack will understand.

"I've got some demands for the big guy."

He raises an eyebrow and holds out his hand. "I might have to see your list."

"Sorry, top secret." I shuffle into a quick jog toward Santa's area.

He catches up quickly and stops in front of me under a lighted trellis. "Ah, mysterious. I like it." We lock eyes.

"Hey, you're under the mistletoe." A little girl points at us, her blonde curls cascading down her shoulders under a Santa hat.

I look up the green leaves and white berries. Suddenly a shadow covers my view. Nick leans down, inching closer. The aroma of his musky cologne sends my heart into overdrive. I freeze, unable to move a muscle. His lips part and descend toward mine. Oh my God. I tremble although heat rages through my veins. He brushes a hand across my cheek.

I gasp and take a step back. My foot hits a patch of ice. The next second my butt slides against the sidewalk. Fire scorches across my face. Guess my body went into self-defense mode. One kiss from Nick Shaw and I'd never be the same.

"You okay?" He holds out a hand.

I've got to get out of here. I have real plans for my life, real dreams, and law school requires me leaving Hilldale. There's no way I can spend time with Nick and come back from it unscathed. Nope, I need to stick to my original plan, all business.

I nod. "Yeah, but I've got to go. I'll see you at the closing." I take his hand to pull myself up and hightail it to my car, leaving him standing alone under a mistletoe-lined trellis. Yep, I've hit the brink of complete insanity.

CHAPTER FOUR

CELEBRATE GOOD TIMES

I slide the newspaper to the side of the table. Doesn't matter, the image seems to follow me. I can't peel my eyes away. Front page and center, the charity football game complete with the photo of Mr. Green, Mayor Whitman, Nick and me that was taken at half-time. I scan the letters underneath the photo, slowly perusing each letter. "Nick Shaw and guest Holly Clifford." Last time my name was in the paper was in my mother's obituary. For some reason, the churning in my stomach feels the same.

How am I supposed to face Nick today after the way I ran off like my feet were on fire at the tree lighting ceremony? I've got to be the only woman in the history of the world that left Nick high and dry. My best bet is to plead insanity. Especially since the truth is too complicated for me to understand, let alone Nick. It's like all my dreams can come true when he's near me. Dreams I didn't even know I had. Then reality hits hard and I've got to get myself out of the unstable situation. I'm sure Angie heard all about it. Great. Now I get to deal with being mortified and her sarcasm. I can't get out of this town soon enough.

I slug down what's left of my orange juice and pet Jack on the head. "Well, buddy, in about another hour I'll be out of this situation and we'll be on track to move on to bigger and better things."

Jack purrs and slowly blinks at me.

If this weren't the deal of my life I'd call off sick. Nope, not an option today. Time to put on my big girl panties and get this done. I grab my keys and march to the car. No turning back now.

I take the mountain of paperwork from my desk and head to the meeting room at a snail's pace. Actually more like a sloth—a snail might beat me to the desk. I pull open the door and clutch the paperwork to my chest.

Nick leans back in the leather chair. I focus on the fitted blue button-down shirt outlining an array of muscles just dying to burst out from under the fabric. He nibbles at the top of his pen. I stop breathing momentarily.

"Holly, have a seat." Angie gestures toward the empty seat next to Nick. A smirk graces her face.

Why does all the town's gossip have to spread like a pandemic? I slide into the seat, tossing the paperwork on the table.

Nick leans toward me, stopping a few inches from my ear. "Just so you know, I found out your little secret."

I scrunch my eyebrows and turn toward him. "Oh yeah, what's that?"

"The little blonde girl told me. You're on a secret mission helping Santa." He winks.

My stomach flutters. Okay, I can't avoid it anymore. "I'm sorry." I look down at the table, my eyes start to water. Oh, God, pull it together, Holly, you're in a business meeting. Am I more embarrassed or upset? Not that it matters. I've got to tell him something. I run my tongue over my lips. Here goes nothing. I open my mouth to speak.

Angie flips open a manila folder. "Nick, congratulations on your new home. It's a beautiful piece of property, you won't be sorry." She passes out a few forms. "These are Trust Realty's standard contract, irrevocable letter, purchase of sale, and privacy policy. I'll sign first and pass them down."

I close my mouth and swallow hard. Angie is such a control freak. She insists on being present for all signings. Okay, business first. I calculate the math in my head. Once this is all said and done I'm leaving with $22,500. What a great start to my new life. I'll talk to him for a few minutes in the parking lot and thank him for everything. I'll just let him know I'm not ready for anything right now and I'm not one of the use-me-and-lose-me kind of girls. I'll just find a better way of saying it. Maybe I'll have an epiphany.

I take the paper from Angie and sign my name. In one swoop I slide the paper along the table, brushing Nick's fingers during the exchange. Tingles follow the path of his fingers, radiating to my soul. Will I ever feel this way from a touch again?

"Holly, you have the sales agreement and the rest of the paperwork. I'll leave you two to the rest. I've got a meeting with Mr. Green concerning the Holiday Gala. Nick, I'm sure I'll see you there. Enjoy your new property." Angie takes the signed documents and struts out of the meeting room, swaying her hips with each step. Faxing them to the real estate board should take her a few minutes.

Nick taps a pen on the table. "Where do we start?"

More like how do we finish this? I leaf through the top papers and pull out the sales agreement. "You just need to sign and initial every time you see a yellow sticker."

Nick rubs his thumb along my finger during the exchange. "Sounds easy enough."

I pull my hand away, faster than necessary, and knock over half the stack of papers. A few of them float to the floor. *Dammit.* I might as well just throw the keys at him at this point. I bend down to grab the loose papers.

Nick grabs my wrist. "Leave them."

I can't just leave them. I tip my chin up and gaze into his soft brown eyes, full of concern.

"Okay, I'm not buying the secret vigilante gig. What's really going on?" He releases his grip on my wrist.

I sit up in my chair. "I think it's better if we keep everything all business." I nibble my lip.

"Better for whom?" He swivels his chair to face me.

"For both of us. We're going in completely opposite directions. We may never see each other again." Jeez, way to be dramatic. Nothing even happened between us. This whole conversation is a bunch of what-ifs and maybes.

He chuckles. "I'm buying a house in Hilldale. I'm pretty sure we'll see each other again."

I nod. "I plan on leaving. Hilldale's not where I want to be."

He rubs his chin. "And where is it that you want to be?"

Right now…in Nick Shaw's arms with no consequences or regrets, but that's not an answer I wish to share. "Maybe somewhere warmer, down south. I want to go to college, make something of myself. Be someone."

"You *are* someone and you *can* do anything you want, anywhere. So what exactly are you afraid of?"

I cover my face with my hands and drag them down. "My biggest fear is being stuck here—and if I spend any more time with you, I may never leave." Oh my God, that was supposed to stay in my head. All the blood drains from my face.

"Really… that may be the best compliment of my life." He nudges my arm. "You know why I love it here so much?"

I shake my head, trying not to die from embarrassment.

"I travel constantly, meet all kinds of people. Don't get me wrong, it's great, but it's like I'm always in the spotlight. Under a microscope." He runs a hand through his hair. "Not in Hilldale and especially not in the lake house. There's so much privacy, I could probably run around naked and no one would realize."

I muffle a smile. "Don't forget, news spreads like wildfire in Hilldale. If you don't run from it, you may get swallowed up."

"I'll take my chances." He bends down and picks up the papers, placing them on the table. "Does the gossip bother you?"

"I couldn't care less what anyone thinks." Wish that was true.

"Glad to hear it. So now that we both know where we stand, how about we go to dinner to celebrate the closing? You know, just friends or colleagues or however you want to label it. My mother was raving about this new restaurant. Angelo's, I think." He searches my face, waiting for an answer.

I guess he does have a point about the whole gossip ordeal. Nothing wrong with hanging out with him since he knows it's strictly platonic. Guess he wants me to put my money where my mouth is. But Angelo's. Really? It's way out of my price league and it's nearly impossible to get a reservation. It *is* a cause for celebration, though. Maybe hanging out with Nick for a little while longer won't hurt. Like he said, we're both leaving anyway, so no harm done. Why do I feel like this is a bad idea?

"You know, maybe we can go for coffee or something once we get these papers signed. Angelo's is booked for months in advance." I fidget with my fingers.

He pulls his cell phone from his pocket and dials. "No harm in trying." He holds the phone to his ear. "Yes, this is Nick Shaw." He lets out a slight chuckle. "Thank you very much. Listen, I'm in town and was wondering if you had a table for tonight. Maybe around seven?"

Please let it be booked. I'm not sure if I can handle a fancy dinner with Nick, but I can't seem to tell him no.

He winks. "Thank you so much. See you then." He presses his

phone and slides it back into his pocket. "Pick you up at six forty-five?"

You've got to be kidding me, he actually got a table. I guess if you're Nick Shaw, you get anything you want. Must be nice. "I'll meet you there."

"I was hoping to meet Jack. He sounds like a real stand-up guy." He flashes a sexy smile.

"Another time." I don't care if we're BFFs or whatever. There's no need for Nick to see where I live. He'd probably pull another stunt like he did at Kransen's, and I've had enough of his charity.

He pulls a stack of papers from the pile. "Let's get this show on the road."

Ugh, he did it again. Made my brain completely shut off. I should be the one handing him the paperwork. I take the papers from him and arrange them on the table. "Mr. Shaw, please sign here and initial here and here." I point to the spaces with the cap of my pen.

"Yes, ma'am." He obliges, holding back a smile.

I slide the plastic hangers along the metal rack of my tiny closet. No, no, and definitely not. It's useless. In one hour I'll be at the fanciest restaurant in town… naked. I huff and rummage through my skirts and dresses one more time. Not like something new will be hiding behind the overabundance of out-of-date fashions. Worst idea ever; coffee was the way to go.

I hold up a plain black dress, normally the one I wear to funerals, but it'll have to do. Maybe a little jewelry will make it less morbid. I slip out of my sweats and slide on the slinky fabric. Hmm, this could work. I spin around and check it out in the mirror of the triple dresser. Whoa, looks kind of sexy. Maybe this was why Mr. Harris was so friendly at Aunt Lydia's wake.

I peruse the jewelry box and take out a long silver necklace that I usually double. I wrap it around my waist and clip the clasp. Perfect, now it's a fancy belt.

Maybe I should just throw on a business suit. No need to give Nick the wrong idea. Eh, I've never been to Angelo's, nor do I ever expect to be invited again. What's the harm in dressing up a bit? I pull my hair into a loose bun and put on my dangly crystal earrings. Amazing what a little black dress and some jewelry can do. No more frumpy nerd girl—now I actually look like I belong with Nick… even though I don't. Not

that it matters; looks are deceiving and I plan on playing up the illusion tonight.

Oh my God, I'm entering the Pantheon. I strut forward toward the mammoth building boasting a multitude of white pillars and marble steps. Lampposts illuminate the path. The intricate carvings in the stone are reminiscent of Roman sculptures. How amazing. Probably the closest I'll get to Italy.

I navigate up the steps to the heavy wooden door guarded by a doorman. He pulls open the door and gestures for me to enter. I walk along the burgundy carpet of the foyer. Wow, it's like I'm at the Oscars in Venice. Crystal chandeliers hang from the ceiling painted like the Sistine Chapel. Lampposts line the perimeter of the room, complete with greenery. A wine chiller sits at every table. Ah, everything I love about Italy, well what I imagine Italy to be like, all in one room. I step up to the mahogany desk and am greeted by a smiling woman.

"Do you have a reservation, ma'am?" She leafs through a leather-bound notebook.

Oh no, where's Nick? I glance around the foyer to try and glimpse through the archway into the dining room. "Umm, yes."

She raises an eyebrow.

"I mean…"

"She's with me," a voice calls from behind me.

I spin to the right. My stomach drops to the floor. Nick stands before me, his hands in the pockets of perfectly tailored black pants. The slate-gray shirt flaunts an array of muscles. My pulse rate triples. Nick in a high-end custom suit is like porn. Man candy at its finest. I sweep him from head to toe, unable to speak. I'm in serious trouble tonight.

He walks toward the desk. "Reservation for two under Nick Shaw."

The hostess's face lights up as if she just met a movie star. "Right this way, please."

I fiddle with my fingers, clutching my small black purse. Maybe I should've researched gourmet cuisine so I have chance of figuring out what to order. With my luck I'll be eating brains… or worse.

The hostess sits us in a private area near the back of the restaurant. "Your waiter will be right with you."

Nick pulls out my chair. I slide onto the soft fabric and scoot closer to the table. He walks around to his seat, my eyes glued onto him with every movement.

A painting of Venice graces the wall behind Nick, adding to the charm. The dim lights reflect off the crystal water goblets, creating an array of rainbows along the white linen tablecloth. A single candle burns in a crystal vase in the middle of the table. Everything about this place is so romantic, it's a miracle you don't fall in love as soon as you walk through the doorway.

"So what do you think?" Nick leans across the table, his face glowing in the candlelight.

Butterflies swarm in my stomach. "Completely perfect." I nibble on my lip.

"Wow, I was going for nice." He flashes that sexy smile. "Did I mention you look absolutely beautiful? I may have to use my tackling skills tonight."

What does that mean? "Excuse me?"

He holds up his hands. "I mean to protect you from a stampede of guys vying for your affection." He lowers his hands to the table. "I know. We're out celebrating as friends." He sips his water. "You're still gorgeous, though."

A flush creeps from my cheeks to my ears. "Thanks, you're looking pretty good yourself." I lock my eyes onto him like a lion eyeing a zebra.

"Welcome to Angelo's. I'm Giuseppe. Your wish is my command." A waiter with a strong accent breaks my trance. He hands us each a menu.

"Good to know." Nick winks.

Hmm, was he talking to me or Giuseppe? I peel my eyes away and focus on the menu. Thank God, I know at least half of these dishes. Maybe something on the lighter side, since my stomach jumps every time I look at Nick. Guys like him should come with a warning label: Contents May Be Hot.

"Want to split an appetizer?" Nick taps his fingers on the menu.

What's with him tonight? He seems nervous all of a sudden, not the confident football god I'm used to. Maybe he realized the commitment of owning a million-dollar property. Yeah, that's probably it.

"Sure, I'm up for trying anything." Yep, that sounded better in my head. "I mean you pick the appetizer."

"We'll try the *capesante al forno*." Nick sets the menu on the table.

Giuseppe steps forward. "Excellent choice, and for the main course?" He shifts his focus to me, then back to Nick. "Sir, will you be ordering for the lady?"

Nick slightly shakes his head. "Wish I could, but I'm still trying to figure her out." He smirks.

Why does this feel more like a date with every passing second? I clear my throat. "I'll have the eggplant *rollatini*."

Giuseppe nods. "And for the gentleman?"

"Chicken Milanese." He hands the menu to Giuseppe. "And a bottle of *moscato*."

"Of course." Giuseppe flashes a quick smile and scurries off.

Looks like we're both unaccustomed to the fancy menus. No reason to take risks with food, especially when you're extremely hungry. Guess I was so edgy, I forgot to eat lunch. Maybe I'm not the only nervous one.

Nick bounces his knee under the table, shaking the floor. "Maybe I should've ordered champagne, since we're celebrating."

Does he think dropping a ridiculous amount of money impresses me? From his track record so far, I guess so. He picked the wrong girl if that's his plan. "Moscato's great. I prefer sweet wines anyway."

Giuseppe sets the appetizer, which I can barely pronounce, on the middle of the table. "Enjoy." He swiftly walks away.

We both stare at the plate, neither one of us sure what to say. Um... I think Jack's canned cat food is a bigger portion than this.

Nick bites at his lip. "Maybe the appetizers aren't meant for sharing." He pokes one of the two small scallops covered in parmesan cheese.

I stick my fork into the one closest to me. "One for each of us." I pop it into my mouth. Mmm, it's like heaven on a cloud. So delicious. Too bad it's so tiny I could eat at least forty of them.

Nick shovels his scallop into his mouth. "Damn, it's awesome." He moves the loose pieces of cheese around the plate. "Too bad it didn't multiply in there."

I let out a small chuckle. "Now we won't be stuffed for the main dish."

Giuseppe returns with a bottle of wine. He pours two glasses, sets the bottle in the chiller, and removes our empty plate. "Did you enjoy?"

We both nod.

"I have a confession to make." Nick fidgets with his fingers.

"Oh, and what's that?" Oh boy, where's he going with this?

"I might have stretched the truth a little about the perfume." He looks down at the table then back up at me.

Yeah, you think? Even Santa's Christmas list isn't that long. "Why would you do that?" Here it comes. He's about to tell me it was his good deed for the holiday season.

"Because I wanted you to win."

"That's cheating. I should've refused your sale." Except for the fact that I need the cash and I wanted to prevail. Janice always wins every contest. Sure, most of it's due to flirting and schmoozing, but for once I wanted the glory. "Why did you want me to win so badly?"

"You deserve it." He sips the wine. "And I was secretly trying to impress you."

I knew it. Of course he had an ulterior motive. Okay, so I thought it was pity, but he wanted to get into my pants. Should I be furious or flattered? Five years ago I would've died right here from a heart attack if I found out I had a shot with Nick. Getting involved with him now would change my whole outlook and goals, and I didn't want that. Maybe another time in another life.

"Ah, money, the root of all evil. Don't you realize I'm not that kind of girl?"

"I do now." He slugs down his wine. "So, what is it that you like?"

"Since we're hanging out as friends, I'll tell you the secret." Guess I could've been a bit more subtle. "A guy who can impress me without spending a dime. Real women can't be bought." I raise my glass and take another sip of the sweet wine.

"A challenge. I like it." He pours another glass of wine.

Dammit. It wasn't supposed to be a challenge, just a fact. This should be interesting, since Nick's the most competitive person I've ever met.

Giuseppe chimes in, placing plates covered in silver domes in front of us. "*Buon appetito.*"

The aroma of fresh tomatoes and garlic fills the air. My mouth waters. Is it from the food or Nick? At this point, I don't think I can satisfy either appetite. Giuseppe lifts our domes at the same time and then takes them away to the kitchen.

Nick's eyes widen. I lower my gaze and stare at the tiniest piece of eggplant I've ever seen. I shift my focus to Nick's plate, which contains about four ounces of chicken placed in the middle of a plate decorated with a variety of sauces. Nick and I burst into laughter at the same time.

He stabs the chicken with his fork, picking up the entire piece. "I think I got a peep."

I cover my mouth, laughing underneath, then slowly lower it down my chin.

My eggplant looks like a sliver, filled with a teaspoon of cheese. "Want to share mine?" I erupt into a mess of giggles.

He holds up his hands. "Maybe my mom was on a diet when she raved about it." He cuts his chicken cutlet in half and eats it in two forkfuls. "I'm still hungry."

I shovel my eggplant into my mouth. "The feeling's mutual."

"About time there's a mutual feeling." He winks. "What do you say to a tray of pizza at Josie's?"

Oh God, Josie's on a Saturday night? Half the town will be there. If I walk in with Nick, I can just see the headlines now. Not that it really matters, since we were already in the paper together. Maybe I should leave well enough alone. "How about we grab a coffee sometime?"

He gulps down his wine and tosses his napkin onto his plate. "No way, I need to make this up or I won't be able to live with myself."

Nick waves at our waiter. "Giuseppe, check please."

"It's not a big deal. Don't worry about it." I finish my wine.

"You don't want to be blamed for my demise, do you?" He

flashes a sexy smile. "One drink and some pizza at Josie's. You might even have fun." He raises his eyebrows.

It's like there's an angel on one of my shoulders and a devil on the other. My rational mind knows I should just go home and nuke a microwave meal, but I may never get a chance like this again. What the hell, one drink and a pizza. What's the worst that could happen? "Okay."

CHAPTER FIVE

JOSIE'S CAFÉ

My heart pounds, keeping perfect time with my heels clicking against the pavement. Unbelievable. Not even one open parking spot left in the jam-packed lot. Nick walks alongside me slowly. Guess he wants to take it easy on that injured hamstring. Works for me, I'm in no hurry to be gawked at anyway.

It'll be nice to see Josie again, though. She and Mom were inseparable back in the day. Even in Mom's last days, Josie was there bringing her milkshakes from Hilldale Dairy. Maybe I should've taken Josie up on all those offers to come up for dinner and on the holidays. I've never met a more giving person. Isolation seemed easier at the time. Guess I'll just add it to my list of regrets.

Nick reaches for the door handle. I take a deep breath and slowly exhale. Now or never. He pulls open the heavy wooden door and gestures for me to enter. I stand in the doorway, sluggishly lifting my eyes. *Great.* Just about every set of eyes in the crowded room stares, their gazes burning through me.

I close my eyes for a split second and then quickly open them. A friendly face blocks out all the others.

"Holly, sweetheart, is that you?" Josie wraps her arms around me, squeezing tight. She takes a step back. "Let me get a look at you." She sweeps her eyes from my face to my black heels. "Gorgeous, like a movie star."

Nick glances over my shoulder. "Hey, Josie."

She grabs his face with both hands and kisses his cheek. "Nick, congratulations." She shifts her focus from Nick to me, then back to Nick. "Did you two come here together?"

I nod.

Her rosy cheeks upturn into the warmest smile. "Come on, drinks are on me."

We follow Josie to the bar and slide onto the black leather stools. I swallow hard, trying to compose myself. Why did I think avoiding Josie was best? She puts the silver lining on any cloud in the sky. Maybe it's because she reminds me so much of my mother. Guess I just couldn't take the memories at the time. Now, I welcome them. Looks like Josie may be seeing more of me after tonight.

"What's your poison?" Josie stands behind the bar. The white lights shining down from the ceiling illuminate her short blond hair.

"I'd kill for a beer and a pizza." Nick flashes those puppy dog eyes that can bring any girl to her knees.

Josie nods and puts her hand over mine. "How about you?"

I put my hand over hers. "I've missed you."

"Me too, sweetheart. Hope you come around more often."

I nod and flick a stray tear from my eye. "I promise." I clear my throat and pull myself back into the moment. "How about a grape martini and an extra plate for some of his pizza."

"Coming right up." She spins around and mixes up a concoction.

"You okay?" Nick rubs his thumb along my shoulder.

Shockwaves shoot across my skin. I don't even flinch. "Yes." For the first time this year it's the truth.

Two guys holding mugs of beer come up to Nick, occupying his attention.

Josie places my drink in front of me. "You two together?"

"Just for tonight." I sip my drink. *Dammit.* Why does everything I say sound better in my head? "I mean we're just friends."

"You sure about that?" Josie winks. "Pizza will be a little bit. Oh, and there's a band tonight." She moves down the bar to wait on other patrons.

I nod. Right now, I'm not sure about anything. Of course, I have my future planned and I'm sticking to the agenda, but this moment isn't accounted for.

I jump down from the bar stool and slide my fingers along Nick's shoulder. "Are you up for a game of pool?" I whisper, inadvertently grazing my lips along his lobe.

"You bet." He swings around, beer mug in hand, and hops off the stool.

I take my drink and head toward the pool table. "Stripes or solids?"

He slugs his beer. "Have you ever played?"

Okay, just once and I was sixteen. "Not in a while." Still the truth.

He sets his beer on a nearby table and racks the balls. "I'll break. First sunk ball decides who's what."

So, maybe we didn't really play by the rules.

He carefully removes the metal triangle, keeping the balls as compact as possible. He places the cue ball on the black dot and leans against the table. Holy hell! The outline of his muscles dances underneath that shirt with every move. I can't peel my eyes away. Who would want to? A loud *thud* resonates through the air.

He removes the cue stick from the table. "I'm solids."

At this point he could tell me he's rainbow polka dots and I'd have to believe him. Not like I saw anything move but his hot body. I take a pool cue and rub some blue chalk on the tip. At least I can pretend I know what I'm doing. I walk around the table, dragging the cue behind me. Hmm, I've got it. "Green-and-white ball in the corner pocket." Pretty easy shot, I should make it. I lean over the table. A few whistles break my concentration.

Nick glares around the room, trying to find the source of the noise. He folds his arms across his chest, accentuating his impressive pecs.

Cute. Is he offended or jealous? Either way, it's flattering. I shift my weight and tap the cue ball with just enough force. It smacks off the green-and-white ball, sending it into the pocket.

A row of guys lean against the far wall and watch. "Nice," one of them says.

I walk around the table and find another easy shot. "Blue-and-white ball, left corner pocket." I tap the cue ball, sending the blue-striped ball into the pocket.

"Time out." Nick makes the time-out sign with his hands and steps forward, wedging me against him and the pool table. "Why do I feel like I'm being hustled?"

I wiggle to the side, creating some space between us. "Beginner's luck." I shrug. Amazing I'm even the least bit focused. Maybe my brain realizes I need to direct my attention on something other than Nick. I take another swig of my martini and peruse the table. Guess my luck's running out, no easy shots. I lean over against the table, almost hitting Nick with my hip.

"Pizza's ready," Josie shouts.

I skip the cue ball off the table, sending it rolling across the floor.

A guy from the back wall steps up. "My turn next?" He raises an eyebrow.

Nick snatches the ball from his hand. "Thanks, I'll take it from here."

I chuckle and follow Nick to a table near the corner, where Josie left our pizza. I plop into the chair. "What was that about?"

He shakes his head. "He's trouble. Nothing you want to get involved with."

"Really?" I turn and glance over my shoulder. "Isn't that Bobby from the dairy farm?"

Nick rips into a piece of pizza. "Yeah, flipped a tractor in a stupid game of chicken."

"Uh, in the ninth grade." I bite my pizza.

He shrugs. "He's still the same."

Nick hasn't been here in years. No way he'd know what Bobby's like nowadays. "When's the last time you two talked?"

He huffs. "Who the hell cares?" He tosses the crust on the tray. "Tonight's about you and me celebrating. Bobby's not invited to the party."

I laugh. "Okay. Tonight I'm all yours." And I've done it again.

I blink, trying to focus my blurry vision. Amazing, just when I think he can't get any sexier, he goes and does this. Nick flings a guitar strap over his shoulder and joins the local band up on stage.

"Give it up for our own football star, Nick Shaw," the lead singer says into the microphone.

A roar of clapping fills the air. I sway from side to side, steadying myself against the back of the chair. I take a sip of my third martini.

"For those of you don't know, Nick used to be the guitar player of Steel Asylum back in the day." The singer runs a hand through his hair and nods to the other members.

Hoots and hollers fill the bar.

Beautiful, familiar chords flow through. The crowd breaks into a frenzy. I close my eyes, taking in the melodic tones. Even in my altered state, it hits me. Oh my God, they're going to attempt "Stairway to Heaven"?

I gaze at the stage, following Nick's every move. His fingers glide along the strings effortlessly. Like everything he touches turns into pure magic. The lights shine down, glowing all around him, turning him into an angel.

My eyes lock onto him, refusing to take in anything else. The singer belts out the lyrics, trying to capture Robert Plant's essence. Of course it's not even close to perfect, but it's fun. Maybe that's the point.

Nick's fingers tap along the strings. His forearm muscles dance along the rolled-up sleeves of his gray dress shirt. What is it about musicians and athletes that drives me wild? And the combination, that's just like an atomic bomb about to go off. Willpower, where are you?

I chair dance to the final chorus, Nick still in my crosshairs. The lights dim, casting a blue glow over the small stage. Nick slides his fingers along the strings. Perfect finish. The crowd cheers, giving a standing ovation. Nick tosses the guitar strap back over his head and sets the Les Paul Starburst down. If he carried that in one hand and a football in the other, no doubt he'd get mauled to death with every step. The foursome of bandmates and Nick walk to the front of the stage and take a quick bow.

"Don't even think of going anywhere. We'll be back after a quick break. Here's more Zeppelin to rock your world." The lead singer steps away from the mic and switches to a CD.

Nick slides into the chair at our table. "What's the verdict?"

Is he for real? He turned from hot football player to smoldering rock god in a matter of five minutes. I'd say the jury's unanimous. "I didn't know you had a secret talent."

He leans forward across the table. "More where that came from." He sits back in his chair.

I sip my drink. "Maybe it's time I learn some of them." Wait, did that just slip out of my mouth? I set down my glass. Enough of the liquid confidence. Or is it truth serum?

He raises an eyebrow, flashing a quick smile. "You know, I've never met anyone like you."

"I guess you don't get out much."

He sips his beer. "Seriously, you're... real."

I slug down the rest of my martini. "There's nothing worse than being surrounded by fake smiles and judging eyes. I can relate."

He shakes his head. "It's not that. You're focused but can still see the whole picture. A sweetheart but not a pushover. And you never let your guard down, even when you should."

"That's how you end up getting hurt."

He slides his hand across the table, running his thumb along my fingers. "Or it's how you find something amazing. It's all about taking a risk, and I'd risk anything to be with you right now."

My heart pounds like a jackhammer. Never in my wildest dreams did I think someone would say that to me, let alone Nick. Guess it's now or never, go for it or stop it dead in its tracks. What the hell?

I lean forward and interlock my hand with his. "What's stopping you?"

His eyes widen. He pushes out the chair and walks around the table to me. I lock onto his caramel-brown eyes. He leans forward, moving in slowly. Oh my God, it's really happening. I never thought people got to live out their ultimate fantasy. Sometimes I love being wrong.

He tucks a strand of hair behind my ear and brushes his cheek against mine. "Ask me that when you're sober."

I sigh. Ugh, sucker-punched. "I haven't had that much to drink."

"You're not driving. I'm taking you home." He holds out his hand.

I huff and take it. Too bad he's not taking me home, as in

spending the night. Like I'll ever have a chance like this again. Guess I got my wish, just friends. Why on earth did I think that was a good idea?

"The white one at the end of the street." Maybe he won't notice the chipped paint and cracked sidewalk in the dark. I tap my fingertips on the armrest of Nick's black Mustang. So much for keeping him away from my house. One look at the tattered siding and dilapidated steps, and he'll have a construction crew here in the morning. No thanks, I've had enough of the Nick Shaw Recovery Fund. Guess nothing tonight is going as planned.

Nick pulls up to the curb and shuts down the engine. "Let me walk you to your door."

I shake my head and open the car door. "I'm fine. Thanks for tonight." I step onto the sidewalk and shut the door.

Nick jumps out of the car. "No way, I've got to get you home safe."

"Mission accomplished." I walk toward the steps.

Nick darts to my side, catching up with me instantly. "Are you always this difficult?"

"What's that supposed to mean?" Aren't I making it easier for him?

He shrugs. "You never let anyone help you... with anything. Why?"

Odd question. Why would I want to rely on everyone else? "I don't need help getting home."

"Everyone needs help with something." Nick stops at the edge of the concrete steps.

"Yeah, what do you need help with? It seems like you've got it all figured out." I walk up the three steps to my porch. Nick follows suit.

He steps forward and takes my hand. I turn and look up, stopping inches from his lips. The aroma of musky cologne mixed with beer fills the space between us. Sexiest smell ever, didn't see that one coming.

He slides his hand along my cheek. "I can't stay away from you."

The hell with logic and rational thinking. So he doesn't fit into the mapped-out future plan, big deal. The future's not here yet and tonight, right now, I want him. We can worry about tomorrow later. "So don't." I rest one hand on his waist and slide the key in the lock with the other.

Nick presses his lips against mine, moving forward at the same time the door gives. We step into my house lip-locked. He slides his hand down to the back of my neck, weaving his fingers through my hair.

I glide my hands up, feathering the curves of his sculpted muscles on the way. I imagined this moment in my mind for years, never thinking it might actually happen. Amazing, so much better than I ever dreamed. Who would've thought reality beats fantasy?

Nick kicks the door closed, leaving the cold behind us. Not that it matters, hellfire doesn't hold a candle to the scorching flames burning through me. The kisses grow more passionate by the second. I navigate backward, guiding Nick up the stairs. The bedroom's just a short distance away.

My God, I've never had a man in my bedroom before. In fact, it's been years since I've been with anyone. Nick's been with tons of women. I mean, all through school they threw themselves at him. Now, it's probably magnified tenfold. Am I ready for this?

Soft kisses travel from my lips to my neck. Blood rushes through my veins. I press my body against his, trying to erase any distance between us. Who am I kidding? I've been ready for this my whole life, and for once, I'm not letting the opportunity pass me by.

Nick nibbles on my earlobe. "Which way?"

"Follow me." I slide my hand down his chest to his fingertips. Hooking a finger around his, I walk forward and open the door.

The moonlight from the window shines along his chiseled jawline, sending silver starlight through the natural highlights in his hair. Ah, pure perfection. I freeze for a split second, admiring the view. Reality hits me hard. No reason to waste any more time. I lunge forward, smacking my lips against his. Passion erupts from the pit of my stomach, taking over.

The seductress inside bursts out full force. Intense energy flows through, turning my PG kisses into a frenzy of triple-*X* desire. Never thought I had it in me, but Nick turns me into a different woman, one I didn't know existed.

I slowly unbutton his shirt, tracing patterns on his skin after each one gives. Finally, the last one comes undone. I tug at the shirt, pulling it off his body. Wow, what a body. I take a step back, feasting my eyes on the man candy.

He steps forward and unzips my dress in one quick motion. It falls to the floor, revealing my black bra and panties. Nick lifts me up, breaking my trance. I wrap my legs around his waist and slide my fingertips along his bulging biceps. He marches toward the bed, slowly lowering me onto the soft comforter. I can't wait to have him, yet I want this moment to last forever. Eternity takes way too long. I scoot up on the bed. Nick crawls forward, predatory instincts taking over. My stomach drops. *Dammit.* How could my nerves get the best of me at a time like this? *Get it together, Holly.*

I swallow hard. Okay, so maybe I'm not even close to as experienced as Nick. Hunger fills his eyes. I doubt it matters at this moment. He's mine for tonight. He traces his fingers from my belly to my breasts, and goose bumps follow the path. He leans down and presses his lips against mine, his hand cupping my breast. He draws down the straps and unhooks the back with one click of his fingers. Ah, his magic fingers. This is nothing like prom, when I thought I was being probed. He forms small circles around my nipples with his fingers. Nick clearly understands the needs of a woman. I let out a slight moan. I navigate down the bumps of his body, and stop at the button of those custom dress pants. I snap my fingers around the clasp, opening a realm of intense possibilities.

The zipper slides down from the force of his throbbing body. Amazing, more impressive by the minute. He moves his hips, knocking the pants off, and kicks them to the floor. The silk fabric of his boxers sweeps against my moist skin. A kaleidoscope of butterflies flutter in my stomach.. No matter what, this night goes down as unforgettable.

He slips out of the boxers and hovers above me, lowering his body until he's pressed against me. My breath quickens. Now or never. He hooks a finger around the strap of my bikini panties, dragging them down my hips. I arch my back, helping him in the journey.

I gasp. We need protection. Hope those condoms I put in my night stand just in case have a long expiration date. Nick moves a finger along my thigh, up to my nether regions. My body goes into overdrive. I've got to focus before my brain shuts itself off and I give in. I reach up to the nightstand and pull a packet out of the drawer, passing it to Nick.

He takes it with his teeth, ripping open the foil wrapper. He slides the sheath on and glides his lips over mine, pressing against me at the same time. Animal instincts take over. Whatever doubt once resided inside me disappears. I move forward, allowing my body to engulf him. Slow and steady, he fills me completely.

We move in a perfect rhythm, as if we know just what the other is thinking. I run my fingers along the peaks and valleys of Nick's back up to his hair, tangling my fingers into the strands. I moan louder as my pleasure grows. He swerves his hips with every thrust, driving my body wild. Intense passion builds inside. My breath quickens. Oh God, I can't take it anymore. I dig my fingers into his back, releasing my desire. Fireworks shoot through me, erupting in every cell of my body. Nick moves faster, sending my sensitive body into hyper-speed. His sweaty skin glistens in the moonlight. He buries his head in my shoulder and lets out a groan, erupting inside me. I skyrocket into another dimension. Earth-shattering doesn't even begin to describe what just occurred.

We both roll over and catch our breath. Amazing. There's no other word for Nick. Completely perfect in every way. Sure, I've read about nights like this and can recall scenes from chick flicks, but never in reality.

Nick wraps his arm around me. I nuzzle into his chest, closing my eyes and replaying the events of tonight in my mind. Slowly, I drift off into dreamland, which can't compete with reality at this moment.

Soft kisses move along my cheek. Feels more like sandpaper. The hum of an engine vibrates my chest.

I run my fingers through Jack's soft fur and place him next to me. "I guess someone's hungry."

"Starved." Nick stretches.

I chuckle. "I meant Jack, but I make a mean omelet."

Nick scratches Jack's ears. "Jack, we finally meet." Jack rubs against Nick's cheek, purring. Nick rolls out of bed and slides on his boxers. "I'll make the coffee."

Sweet Jesus. The image of Nick standing shirtless in my bedroom with sun glaring off his body should be carved into stone.

"You coming?" He puts on his clothes from last night.

I nod, pulling myself back into reality. "I'll meet you in the kitchen." I throw on black yoga pants and a T-shirt then head downstairs.

Should I say something? Maybe tell Nick what a great time I had. Not that he didn't figure it out. Never been in this situation before, guess I'll follow his lead.

I grab a pan from the cupboard and some eggs, cheese, mushrooms, and ham from the fridge. "What would you like?"

He makes two cups of coffee in the Keurig and takes them to the table. "I'd like to take you out on a date."

Oh God, I slept with him on the first date. Real classy. "Didn't we just go on a date yesterday?"

He shakes his head. "Nope, you said that was strictly friendly." He muffles a smile. "I'm pretty sure we're best friends."

I throw a potholder at him, hitting him in the arm. "I meant in your omelet."

"I like everything." He sips his coffee. "So?"

"What?" I crack the egg in the pan and add the ham and mushrooms.

"Holly, will you go out with me tomorrow night?" He nibbles on his lip.

How can I resist his charm? Okay, going out with Nick again sort of complicates things. I mean, when do we stop, when we both leave? It's not like long-distance relationships are easy, and neither one of us should give up what on what we want.

One more date can't hurt anything. Plus, after last night it would be strange to say no. I put down the spatula on the counter. "I'd love to."

His smile lights up the room. "Wear something warm, it's the Winter Carnival."

What is it with him and public events? Dates should be secluded and romantic. I'm clearly not a trophy or something he wants to show off. Maybe he really loves the holiday festivities. Sometimes I feel like I'm trapped in a Norman Rockwell painting. Seeing Josie again would be fun, and the mayor and library board are a great group of people. Oh God. He's doing something to me I never imagined was possible. Making me like this town. Great. More complications.

CHAPTER SIX

WINTER CARNIVAL

Hope I don't drop a glass slipper on the way home, or is *fuzzy boot* more appropriate? I'm clearly losing my mind. The days of hiding in the shadows are over. Now the spotlight shines directly on me. Well, on Nick and me whenever we're together. Never thought I'd like it so much. History shows everything great never lasts. So when does this fractured fairy tale end?

The doorbell resonates through the air like an angel's choir. Oh well, forever's overrated. Time to live for the moment. I run a hand through my blond curls and take one last glance in the mirror. The silver spread through my blue sweater dress sparkles in the soft light like icicles. Perfect for tonight. My first official date in… too long to remember. I walk through the foyer and pull open the door.

"You look great, Rookie." He holds out a bouquet of white roses dipped in blue and silver glitter with a few plastic snowflakes set in the arrangement. "Hope the ice sculptures don't melt when you walk by."

I roll my eyes, sporting an ear-to-ear grin. "How long did it take you to come up with that one?"

"'Bout an hour." He holds out a hand. "Your chariot awaits."

I set the flowers in a vase on the small table of the foyer, throw on my coat, and take his hand. A soft gust of cool air rushes across my skin on the way outside. I take in the cool, crisp scent of winter. Millions of stars light up the night sky, twinkling like diamonds. I've been on this date for less than a minute, and it's already the best one of my life. Not that I have much to compare it to. I nuzzle into Nick, following him along the cracked sidewalk. He stops in front of a souped-up white Hummer and holds open the passenger door for me.

I climb in. "Nice car."

"More horsepower than a chariot." He fires up the engine and we're off.

Looks like he's pulling out all the bells and whistles tonight. *Please don't let me wake up if I'm in the midst of a dream.*

Almost every house on the five-mile ride to the Winter Festival at the lake boasts displays of lights and Christmas scenes, like living in the North Pole. Even the Grinch couldn't help cracking a smile. Why was it that I stayed away from the yearly festivities? Ah, not a fan of dredging up old memories. Maybe it's time to make some new ones.

Nick turns on the radio, quickly finding a channel with Christmas music. "You into the spirit yet, or do I have to send some ghosts to visit you tonight?"

I raise an eyebrow. "Funny." Guess I forgot the joy of the holiday season. It only took an NFL player that all the girls obsess over to show me the error of my ways. Probably more realistic than angels or ghosts. "Maybe you're a ghost of Christmas."

He shakes his head. "Nope. Once in college I tried walking through a wall after partying too hard at the frat house. Didn't work out so well."

We both chuckle.

A grove of lighted trees line the banks of the lake, shining into the heavens. Nick pulls into the cobblestone driveway of his lakeside mansion. "Can't wait to move in here. It's going to rock, especially at this time of year."

I nod. Best property in all of Hilldale. What's it like to be Nick Shaw? To get everything you've ever wanted. Sure, he worked for it, but some people work forever and never get what they truly desire. Maybe some of his mojo will rub off on me.

"You ready to hit the carnival?" He steps out of the car around to the passenger side, opening the door.

As ready as I'll ever be. "Bring on the candy canes and cocoa."

He takes my hand, interlocking our fingers. "I like your enthusiasm."

We walk along the moonlit path, hand in hand. Pretty soon a mob of people will surround Nick, shaking his hand and wishing him luck. I've finally gotten past the awe and his hotness factor, but it's almost like I'm walking in with royalty. No way to keep the night just between the two of us. Our first official date includes me and half the town. Guess he doesn't have it all. Living under a microscope has its downfalls. Never thought I'd be under it with him.

The path opens to a large field, now turned into a winter wonderland. White lights adorn a multitude of stands selling everything from hot cocoa to roasted peanuts. Christmas music flows through the air, and Santa strolls along, handing out candy canes. A few people ice skate along the shallow portions of the lake. There's even a horse and carriage taking people on a ride along the banks of lake. I focus on the white horse. Last time I was on a horse-drawn carriage was back when I was twelve at the Cape. Mom insisted it's the best way to see the Victorian homes up close. Boy, was she right. One of the best vacations of my life.

"You up for a ride?" Nick breaks my trance.

At this point I'm up for anything, and a moonlit romantic ride with Nick tops my list. "Sure." That's all I can say, since *God, yes* doesn't seem appropriate.

We walk toward the carriage.

Jim Reynolds, the owner of 5 Star Stables, waves to us. "Nick, you and your girl want a ride?"

Nick nods and shakes Jim's hand. "Keep her at a slow trot. Don't want to scare Holly."

Is he for real? "The horse can't possibly drive as crazy as you." I pet the top of her mane, careful not to disturb the blue and silver ribbons tied to the end of a few strands of braided hair. What a beautiful, pristine animal. "What's her name?"

"Snowflake. Perfect for the holiday season. ?" Jim sets a bucket of water in front of Snowflake. She takes a long drink.

Perfect has become the theme for my life these past few weeks. I climb up onto the step of the carriage. Nick glides his hand along the back of my thigh. His fingers grip around my charcoal leggings, almost cupping my butt. My pulse skyrockets. Is he trying to help me or has this night already taken an erotic turn? I push forward at warp speed and jump into the seat. Nick slides in next to me.

He takes the thick blanket from the edge of the seat and drapes it over us. "Look around, how could anyone want to leave this place?" He wraps an arm around me.

I glance around at the clear night sky gleaming with starlight. The lighted path has a hint of fallen snow along the sides. He's right about the serene beauty. But it comes with a price just like anything else. "Maybe because there's not much opportunity. You can't live on hopes and dreams."

He nudges me. "Okay, Debbie Downer."

What's his point? He knows exactly how I feel about Hilldale. Well, he knows I want out. Okay, since I've been spending time with Nick, the town has more appeal than it ever did. Still, the fact remains the same. If I don't get out, my dream of law school never comes true. I refuse to work for Angie long-term and live a miserable life. Not anymore, no more wasted time.

. . .

I shrug. "Just a realist."

"You got to admit. It's pretty great this time of year."

I flash a smile. "This is the best time I've had in years." Oops. That just slipped out.

"Right back atcha."

Seriously? He must've sipped too much egg nog, because his whole life seems like a fairy tale. Doubt this is the peak.

"I'm going to enjoy this lake until I start training in July." He fidgets with his fingers. "So what's the master plan?"

Great. How did this date take a serious turn? "It's still up in the air. I'll be sending out my applications next week. I guess I'll see what happens."

"I hear the University of Iowa has a great law program."

He's right, and if I'm accepted, there's a chance I'd go; but I'm not ready to share that information yet. Huh, U of Iowa didn't even make the short list, until now. Maybe there's more heat in the Midwest than down south like I'd originally planned. "Yep, it's one of the top schools." I snuggle closer to Nick, relaxing to the rhythm of the horse's trot. Enough of the serious talk. "What are the chances of getting my hands on some of those hot nuts after the ride?" And I've done it again.

Nick chuckles. "I'll need dinner first."

Heat creeps across my face. My cheeks are probably rosier than Santa's. I try to squirm away but he holds me close.

"It's the Winter Carnival, anything goes." He points to the crescent moon. "Good sign right there?"

"Yeah, nice clear night."

"The moon." He drops his arm back around my shoulders. "When the two horns point to the east, it's a waxing moon, still growing on its way to a full moon."

He's into astronomy too? "Are you turning into a werewolf or something?"

"Maybe later." He flashes a sexy smile. "It means now's the

time to start a new adventure. Cool fact from a mythology class I took in college."

"I'm pretty sure I'm already on one." I rest my head on Nick's shoulder.

The horse slows to a stop. The half-hour ride seemed to go by in the blink of an eye. Guess time really does fly when you're having fun. Nick's here for another six months before he starts training. It'll probably feel like a week. If I stick to my new motto, "Live in the right now," I might have a chance at surviving unscathed. Time to put my money where my mouth is and enjoy the night.

Jim walks over to the side of the carriage and holds out his hand to help me down. "Enjoy the ride?" he asks.

Yeah, I don't want to get off this ride with Nick. I nod.

Nick shoves a few dollars into Jim's hand. "Thanks, Jim. Merry Christmas."

He slides his arm around me and we walk through the field to the main carnival area. "Let's get you some hot nuts." He winks.

Guess I won't be living that one down.

The cool breeze calms the heat surging through my body. Energy surrounds me. I can't remember the last time I smiled so much. Nick breathes new life into my soul. Amazing how things can change so much in a short amount of time.

"Don't you two look cozy?" a voice breaks through.

And there go my happy thoughts. Angie struts up to us. Her hair catching just enough of the breeze to float along her shoulders like she's in the middle of a photo shoot.

She stops in front of us, her chin tipped toward the sky as always. "Guess I'd attach myself to a client who buys a seven-figure listing too."

A low growl forms in my throat. What's she talking about? She made double what I made on the sale. Hate to break it to her, but not all of us are the gold-digger type. Pretty sad, she spends her time dating guys who can give her whatever she wants, yet none of them actually do it. Doesn't she realize she owns Trust Realty and can make her life anything she wants it to be without snagging the next Donald Trump? "What's that supposed to mean?"

Nick squeezes me tighter. Does he think he needs to restrain me? Please, I'm not going start a brawl. I'd like to think we're both more mature than that, although I can't speak for Angie.

"Whatever you'd like it to." She smirks. "Have fun... Oh, Nick, there's a silent auction at the art gallery, in case you want to spread some more Christmas cheer." She flashes a smile and a Miss America wave then takes off toward the art gallery.

I try to remove the hateful thoughts from my body.

"Guess she'll never change." Nick shrugs.

"She could've been yours." God help whoever gets her.

"Yeah, and hell could've frozen over, the world could've been swallowed up by a black hole, and I could've missed meeting the most amazing person I've ever laid eyes upon... you." He leans in and brushes his lips against mine.

My stomach drops to the ground. I weave my fingers through the back of his hair, putting all the passion flowing inside me into this one kiss. Giggles fill the space around us. Well, we are in public, making quite the display. He pulls away slowly.

Two young girls, probably around eight years old, whisper to each other and chuckle. They scamper away. Guess they can't imagine kissing a guy in public without getting cooties. Just let them wait a few more years.

How can he make every second we spend together seem like the best of my life? It's like winning the lottery, eating the best meal you've ever tasted, and being swept off to a tropical island paradise all at once.

We slowly stroll through the carnival, a few people stopping to talk to Nick on the way.

"Nick, win your girl a prize," a game attendant yells through the crowd.

Ah, I love being called Nick's girl. Sweet candy to my ears.

Nick slides his arm from my shoulder to my hand. "You need one of those." He gestures toward the prizes at the Snowball Toss. Winner gets a stuffed polar bear.

"I can honestly say I don't have one." I laugh. So this is what it's like to be carefree. If I can hold onto my feelings from tonight forever, I've lived a full life. Maybe those Christmas magic theories aren't entirely fantasy.

We step up to the stand. Looks like the player needs to hit the abominable snowman in the head with the snowball. Three hits win a plush polar bear.

Nick pulls out a five-dollar bill. "My girl wants a polar bear. Let's get this party started."

Nick just called me his girl too! Oh my God, those words coming from Nick's lips throw my heart into a frenzy. An ear-to-ear grin plasters across my face. I take a deep breath, trying to control my erratic pulse.

A small crowd gathers round, watching Nick in action. He takes the oversized softball and winds up. A flick of his wrist, and the abominable snowman takes a direct hit to the head. A few people clap.

He nods toward me and winks. "One down, two to go." He throws the next snowball, hitting the snowman again.

I bounce on my toes. Who would've thought a silly carnival game could be so exciting? The crowd cheers Nick on as if he's about to win the big game.

He takes the last ball and tosses it up, catching it in his hand. He turns toward me. "If I slay the snowman and win you a polar bear, do I get to take you on another date?"

"Say yes," someone in the crowd yells.

Is he for real? He can take me anytime, anywhere. I nod.

He pulls back his arm and flings the ball forward effortlessly. Amazing. It's like his body knows it was made for sports. The ball smacks off the snowman's head.

"We have a winner!" the game attendant shouts. "A prize for the beautiful lady." He hands me a giant stuffed polar bear. I wrap my arms around it, hugging it to my side. First time a guy ever won a prize for me. In fact, I've never been to a carnival with a guy before. Okay, so I don't have any need for a giant stuffed animal. Who cares? There's just something about Nick slaying the abominable snowman like a gallant knight from back in the day. I'll cherish it forever.

I kiss him on the cheek. "I can't wait to see what's next."

"I've got lots of tricks up my sleeves." He slides his arm around my waist. "Let's get you those hot nuts."

We wander around the different stands, stopping to grab a hot chocolate and some roasted peanuts. The breeze stops, leaving a calm, clear night brightened by twinkling stars and an overabundance of Christmas lights. Complete perfection... I nestle into Nick's shoulder... in every sense of the word.

We stop at the entrance to the art gallery. Nick points toward the glass doors. "Wanna take a look?"

I nod. "Sure." He doesn't seem like an art buff. Thank God. I'd never know the difference between a Picasso and a Rembrandt. I'm just drawn to things I like. One thing in particular at the moment.

We stroll through the gallery, stopping for a few minutes to take in the beauty of each painting. How deceiving. A plain tan building that looks like it could barely hold a small party opens to a giant space, adorned with colorful and inspiring work. In all my years living here, I never made a point to check out the art gallery. Doesn't matter, going anywhere in this town with Nick is like seeing it for the first time.

A collection of about fifteen paintings graces a large wall in the middle of the gallery. A gold box and slips of paper sit on a stand near each one. Ah, guess this is the silent auction. I peruse the various canvases. A winter scene catches my attention, and I stop dead in my tracks. I follow each brushstroke of the masterpiece depicting a large house on a pristine lake. The trees along the side adorned in colorful lights and a snowman guarding the entrance. Did the artist have a vision of Nick's house in the future?

"Beautiful," Nick says. "And I wasn't talking about the painting."

Heat creeps across my cheeks to my ears. "You're crazy."

"Crazy about you." He runs thumb along my fingers. "What do you say about being my date for the Holiday Gala? You already love the gallery."

"Well, since it's for charity." I chuckle. "I'd love to go."

Heels click along the marble tiles. "You'll need some art for that new property." Angie puts her hand on Nick's shoulder.

My stomach clenches. "I think the place is great just the way it is."

"Yes, I'm sure that stuffed animal will add to the décor." She chuckles.

Okay, I've had more than enough of her for one day. "Speaking of which, Nick, can you hold him for me? I'll be right back."

Nick reaches for the bear. "I'll protect him with my life." He gives me a salute.

God, please don't let him ever lose that sense of humor. Seems to be a rare find these days. I wave and make my way to the restroom to get away from Angie for a few minutes..

Wow, all granite and so clean you can eat off the floor. Never realized the art gallery was so elegant. Guess that's why the Holiday Gala is held here every year. I wash my hands and take a quick glimpse in the mirror. Are my cheeks rosier than normal from the winter air or the man who makes me blush every time he flashes that sexy smile? Either way it's a look I like. It's been a while since such color has been breathed into my life.

As much as I hate to admit it, that painting would look perfect mounted on the wall of Nick's lake house. Maybe I should put in a bid. I've got a few extra bucks burning a hole in my pocket. Not that I'd ever win. Who knows? Anything can happen.

I run my fingers through my hair, trying to fix the windblown strands, and then head back to Nick. I turn the corner and slow my pace. Great, Angie's still there. Maybe I can stall until she leaves. I think we've spoken enough for today, or forever, although that's not an option. I linger behind them, waiting for the conversation to end.

"You're going to bid on that painting for her?" Angie folds her arms across her chest.

"Yeah, she loves it." Nick scribbles on a piece of paper, tossing it into the box.

She taps her stiletto on the marble. "Never thought you'd be the type."

He crinkles his forehead. "What's that supposed to mean?"

"At first I thought you were shelling out cash for a charity case, but now…you're a pimp."

"What?"

"You heard me. Actually, it's more like you bought her. Between the house, the stunt you pulled at Kransen's, Angelo's, this painting. That's one expensive date. Guess money *can* buy anything." She steps forward and peruses the painting. "And she's jumping at every dollar you wave."

"Should I get some Mr. T jewelry and a cane?" He chuckles. "You're crazy."

"And a gold grille for your teeth." She lets out a giggle. "While you're buying houses, maybe you can set her up in something halfway decent. I can get you a good deal." She winks.

"What the hell, she can just move into the lake house with me. I'll start a new football reality show: *Pimpin' and Passin'.*"

They both burst out into laughter.

"Or *Gold Digging For Beginners*. She could be the star." Angie flashes a smug smile.

He turns toward me, his eyes wide. "Hey, Rookie, you're back."

Is he seriously joking about buying me like some cheap slut? Gold digger who lives in a dilapidated home? Is that what he thinks? Hate to break it to him, but the girl standing next to him would jump at the chance. Amazing, he and Angie get together and I'm right back in high school being bullied. Not anymore. I've had enough.

I point my finger in his face. "Don't... don't speak another word to me... ever." I rush out of the gallery, tears streaming down my face. I quickly wipe them away. He doesn't deserve my tears.

Hellfire rages through my body. Is this what he thinks? That I'm a gold digger, or worse, a whore? My hands ball into fists, so tight my

fingernails dig in my palms. How could I be so blind? Of course he thinks he can buy whatever he wants. Always worked for him before. Well, not this time. This girl, not for sale.

CHAPTER SEVEN

GRINCH

Why does one of the best times of my life have to turn into one of the worst? I stomp forward through the aroma of fresh-roasted peanuts and s'mores. Not sure where the hell I'm going. As long as it's far away from Nick.

"Holly, will you please wait?"

I glance backward, shooting a death glare. Nick follows right at my heels, even though he's starting to limp. Yeah, like I'm going to feel sorry for him. It's not like he's concerned about *my* feelings. Two seconds with Angie, and I'm the poor outcast who vies for the attention and money of the football hero. Not a chance. Maybe those two should hook up. It seems they're made for each other.

I reach the edge of the grass and look out onto the blacktop. Not a car in sight traveling the dark road. Great, no way home. Typical.

Nick grabs my arm. "Will you please listen?"

I jerk it away. "I think I've heard enough." I fold my arms across my chest.

"We were only kidding around."

So it's okay to degrade and humiliate me with Angie as long as it's all in good fun? Not buying that one. "Yeah, funny."

"It's ridiculous. No truth to any of it." He steps forward, brushing my cheek with his hand.

Any body part that touches me is in danger of being amputated. "I wish that were true." I take a step back.

He crinkles his forehead. "What are you talking about?"

Is he really this blind to his actions? Hot lava runs flows through my veins, creating a path of destruction. Memories of Angie flood my brain, followed by every moment I spent with Nick. Crazy, it's like my life's flashing before my eyes with polluted memories.

I grit my teeth. "You think you can just ride into town and buy up the biggest mansion, woo the townspeople, and have your pick of any woman you want."

He covers his mouth with his hand, laughing underneath. He drops it to his side. "You're making me sound like some gunslinger."

So everything is a joke to him. Guess I'm the laughingstock. "Is something funny?"

His face turns serious. "No, I'm sorry." He nibbles at his lip.

Bastard. Everyone probably thinks the same thing: "Holly's swept away by the handsome, rich, football star. He's probably got one of her in every town." I'm no one's property and I can't be bought.

Everything I've been holding back bursts through. "You have no idea what it's like to care about someone. I mean to truly care about another human being. You think fancy dinners, extravagant gifts, and sharing the spotlight are the way to a girl's heart. Well, you're dead wrong." I wipe away a few tears that fall down my cheeks. "I couldn't care less about any of that. I care about the real Nick. The one who plays guitar with his friends and sings a little off key. Who treats my cat like a member of the family. The one who's not a god. Who's real, with imperfections.

Who made me feel like I'm someone special… up until tonight." I clench my fists then slowly release them.

He runs a hand through his hair and sighs. "I'm sorry."

Really? That's it. Two words can't fix this. I walk away down the street.

"Holly." He grabs my arm. "You're pissed. I get it. Just please let me take you home."

Dammit. It's not like there's an overabundance of cabs in Hilldale, and there's no way I can walk that far when it's this cold. I should've driven myself. Looks like I'm forced to take more charity. "Fine." I trek toward Nick's car, knocking into him as I walk past.

Why do I feel like I'm giving in? I yank open the door and plop into the seat. My eyes fixed on the road ahead like they're locked onto a target. This ride does not mean everything's okay between us. Maybe I should've taken my chances walking. The worst part of all of it, he has no clue how much he hurt me. He doesn't get it, I'm more than pissed. Probably thinks it's my time of the month or something. I knew better but I got involved with Nick anyway. It's my own damn fault.

Nick turns on the radio. "Blue Christmas" blares through the speakers. How appropriate. A week until Christmas and my short-lived fairy tale ends. Looks like I'll be spending another Christmas with Jack. Doesn't matter, we don't need anyone else in our lives anyway. Better off.

Nick puts his hand on my thigh. "Can I at least talk to you?"

I shrug, still looking straight ahead. "It won't change anything."

He pulls his hand away and grips the steering wheel. "I'm not going

to lose you over a stupid comment Angie made and a joke I took too far."

I turn toward him. "You don't get it. It's not just about Angie or what you said, it's about the way you view life. You two live in a different world than I do." I wipe a stray tear from my eye. "You hurt me tonight." I shake my head. "I can't believe I fell for you."

He taps the steering wheel, slowing the car to a stop in front of my house. "I screwed up. How do I fix this?"

I open the door and jump out. "There's nothing you can buy or send that's going to change anything. We're different people who didn't belong together in the first place. Goodbye, Nick." I close the door and run into my house.

I glance down at the screen of my cell phone. Another missed call from Nick. That makes twenty-three calls in less than twenty-four hours. Maybe he finally got the point and regrets last night. Doesn't matter, it's like we're from different planets. Never would've worked anyway. Better to end it before things get complicated. He's leaving in a few months anyway. Who knows, maybe I'll leave Hilldale before he does. New goal: stay as far away from Nick as possible until one of us gets out of this godforsaken place.

No sense in answering if he calls again. Everything's been said. I still can't believe he referred to himself as my pimp. Well, agreed with Angie anyway. The words play in my head like a broken record.

Even though Mom and I never had very much, that's the first time anyone's made me feel cheap. I'll never let another man do that to me again. Jack jumps on my lap and curls up into a compact, furry ball. Amazing. True unconditional love. I run my hand along Jack's soft fur. If only the men of the world could take a lesson.

Enough of the sulking. Time to fix the one thing I do regret. I pick up Jack and set him on the couch. I'm long overdue for a visit with Josie. I brush the few strands of fur from my sweater, grab a coat, and head outside.

The frigid wind whips through, stinging my face. I squint and trek forward, hitting something with my boot. A cardboard box skids across the porch. Hmm, did I order a package? I grab the box and hightail it to my car. I toss the box on the passenger seat and rub my hands together. Crazy, the temperature dropped at least ten degrees in the last few hours. I turn on the engine, waiting a few minutes before cranking up the heat. Ah, a little warmth.

Huh, no address or mailing label. What could it be? I peel off the tape, opening the box in one quick motion. Inside is a CD of Led Zeppelin IV, a football with specks of mud on it, a copy of *The Stand* by Stephen King, and a note that reads, "You'll understand soon. Love, Nick."

I set the box down and rest my head on the steering wheel. A tear streams down my face. Why can't he just let it go? Getting over him will be pure hell. It's not like I'll ever meet anyone else that even comes close to Nick. He found a part of me I didn't know existed anymore. Doesn't matter. It's just not meant to happen. I've got to move on. Nothing more to it. I sigh. Too bad one of us couldn't disappear. Things would certainly be easier.

I read the note over and over again in my mind on the drive to Josie's Café. I used to be great at solving riddles. The only thing I can come up with is Nick murdering me with some type of biological weapon, burying me in the football field, and playing some kick-ass rock music at my funeral. Unless he turned into a psychotic killer, nothing makes sense.

I turn the corner into Josie's parking lot. Amazing, it's close to empty. Maybe because it's 11:00 a.m. I run my fingers along the box one more time, like it's going to give me a sudden epiphany. Nah, this code's way too hard to crack. I need to forget about everything for a while. Some time with Josie just might do the trick.

I rush through the cold air into the warmth of Josie's Café. The aroma of fresh-baked bread and garlic greet me. Just like when I was twelve and skinned my knee a block away, riding my bike. I limped my way to Josie and she hooked me up with a cola, pizza, and a chocolate-chip cookie. In an instant everything was better. Too bad this wound won't be as easily fixed.

Josie spots me almost immediately. Her full rosy cheeks upturn to a smile. "Holly, sweetheart." She rushes up to me, pulling me into a bear hug. "Come sit down. It's great to see you again."

I slide into a small table by the bar. "Yeah, I thought I'd take you up on your offer." I fidget with my fingers.

"You know you're always welcome. What can I get you?"

A time machine so I can travel back three weeks. "Just a cola."

She slides into the seat across from me. "Something wrong?"

It's like she's got a sixth sense. No matter how hard I try, I can never hide anything from her. "It's been a rough few days."

"Let me guess. Does it have something to do with a certain football player?"

I flash a meek smile. "Maybe."

"Do I have to grab the club from behind the bar and scour the town in search of him?" She chuckles.

I shake my head. "It just didn't work out."

She raises my chin. "What happened?"

I shrug. "We're completely different and I don't fit in." My eyes well with tears. "It wasn't meant to be."

"First of all. We're all the same here in Hilldale. No matter who wants to pretend they're better or more exciting, we all come from the same stock." She puts her hand over mine. "Second, don't let anyone make you feel like you don't deserve what you want. You deserve it all."

Amazing. Two minutes with Josie and I already feel better. Of course, if she knew what Nick said, she'd probably clobber him.

"What really happened?"

"He made this stupid comment after Angie referred to me as a prostitute. Something about being a pimp. I overheard them laughing and it set me off." I sigh. "It brought back the awful high school memories."

She shakes her head. "Trust me. I see men acting like asses on a daily basis. For some reason, when they team up with their old friends, it magnifies."

She hit the nail on the head. "We're on different paths. It wouldn't have worked anyway. We're better off ending it now."

"You never know where the road is going to take you. Don't give up on him yet." She slides out of the chair.

"I just want to hide until one of us leaves town. College might finally happen for me."

She puts her hands to her mouth and drops them. "That's wonderful news. I have no doubt I'll be at your graduation someday. Your mom would be so proud."

I look up at her clear blue eyes. "Maybe I could go for a slice of pizza."

"Coming right up. Oh, and a hot chocolate-chip cookie just out of the oven."

My cheeks rise to an all-out smile. "Perfect."

If I could only bottle up some of her positive vibes, I would rid the world of sadness.

She grabs a cola from behind the bar and sets it on the table. "Be right back."

I take a sip and sit back in my chair. Maybe I'll stop up for a visit every once in a while after I head out to college. My applications are almost ready to mail. I'm sticking to the original plan, head somewhere down south where it's warm. Maybe Florida or Virginia. I guess I'll leave it up to fate.

The door opens, ringing a small bell to alert Josie. I look up at the familiar face walking toward me. Great, my horrible luck strikes again. Nick's sister, Gina, walks in with a blonde girl I recognize from high school. I think she was a year behind me.

"Holly, right?" She waves and continues forward.

She doesn't seem like she has a clue as to what's going on with Nick and me. "Hey, Gina."

"I remember you from school," her friend says, "I'm Michelle, Josie's granddaughter. You look amazing. It's been a long time."

How could I forget? Michelle runs the art museum. She's the only person I encountered in school who's just as nice as she is beautiful. I wish Angie would take a lesson from her.

"What's up with my brother? He's been sulking all day."

Oh boy, here we go. I shrug. "I think his leg was bothering him. He must have overdone it at the carnival."

"Makes sense." Two other girls sitting in a booth against the wall holler her name. "Gotta go. Good to see you again."

"Yeah, you too."

"Holly, I'll see you at the gala. I've got your name on the list as a check donor for Trust Realty." Michelle follows Gina.

Dammit. There's no way I'm showing up. That's the one place I can't avoid Nick. Angie can present the damn check herself. She loves the attention anyway. How could she resist being in the spotlight? Ugh, there's one thing that she loves more than being the center of attention. Humiliating me.

CHAPTER EIGHT

HOLIDAY GALA

"Would it kill you to smile? It's an honor to be here, plus you're representing Trust Realty." Angie sips her champagne. "And mingle with everyone, customer service is key." She spots the president of Hilldale Bank, Mr. Philbin, and struts toward him, sporting an obviously fake smile.

It takes more muscles to frown, so maybe I'm giving my face a workout. Does she honestly expect me to be thrilled that I'm here? I've only asked her one hundred times to please present the check herself so I can skip this shindig. Nope, according to her it would cut into the time she needs to make connections. Bullshit. She has lived here forever, and if anyone new moves into town, she's the first one to send a welcome basket. She's not worried about Trust Realty, it's all about making the town adore her. God forbid she's not voted most popular Hilldale resident.

I sigh. I've just got to get through tonight, and I'm in the clear. No more holiday events, Trust Realty closes for a week until January 2, and Jack and I can spend Christmas at home without the threat of running into Nick. Since I still need my job for a little while longer, guess I'd better turn on the charm.

I pat down my blue satin dress, being careful not to knock off any of the silver crystals. Luckily, Josie saved it from her daughter's prom. According to Josie, Angie bragged about the gala for at least an hour to anyone who would listen at the bar. Good thing she mentioned I was presenting the check, even though she only did it in the hopes the information made it back to Nick. Word spreads like wildfire around this town, so I'm sure her plan worked. Josie dropped off the dress the next day, insisting I wear it. So it's retro, still looks great and it's one of a kind. Guess Angie did me a favor by running her mouth.

I grab a glass of champagne from the server's silver tray and slap on a smile. Dozens of people in sleek tuxedos and exquisite dresses talk and laugh in small groupings. Guess I've got to try and be part of a clique. Never thought that would happen in this point of my life. I slug down the rest of my champagne and set the glass on an empty table. Ah, Mr. Green from the library. I'll start with him.

I take another glass of champagne and join his group, examining a painting. "It's nice to see you again, Mr. Green."

"Ah, likewise, Holly." He points toward the colorful piece of art. "What do you think of this piece?"

Great. Of course they want to talk about art. I gaze at the canvas, staring at the ballerina in the deep pink tutu. The subtle brushstrokes along her arms and fingers bring her soul to life. Here goes nothing. "The proportions are true to reality, especially the arch in her back and turn in her neck. She's focused yet invigorated. Like she needs to hold back her excitement even though she wants shout from the rooftops." I sip my champagne.

"Fascinating. I think I love it even more now. I'm bidding on this one." A woman with a diamond the size of a walnut drops a sheet in the silent auction box.

I flash a quick smile. Phew, that went so much better than

expected. Maybe I can make it through this night unscathed. "Enjoy the gala."

Mr. Green nods. "You, as well."

I take a few steps forward and stop dead. Nick floats into the room, a million-dollar smile plastered on his face. My heart races like a ticking time bomb. A perfectly fitted charcoal-gray suit outlines every muscle of his impressive body. Has he ever looked this good? The light reflects off the few silver threads of his green tie with red specks. A little breeze so his hair flows, and I might spontaneously combust.

I've got to keep my distance. No way can my emotions handle both Nick and Angie tonight. I glance up at the clock. Okay, an hour until I present the check. I can avoid him for an hour. If it comes down to it, I can always take the easy road and hide in the bathroom. First step, get him out of my sights. I swing around toward the hors d'oeuvre table, stopping as if I hit a brick wall. Michelle stands a few inches away.

She gasps. "Sorry, didn't mean to sneak up on you. You look amazing."

Normally, I'd think she's just being nice, but for once I feel glamorous. Guess it's her aunt's dress and my up-do. Kind of Old Hollywood chic. Maybe seeing me tonight will make Nick rethink his comment. Okay, he's already apologized and claims to regret it. Regardless, tonight I'm not the nerdy outcast. For the first time ever I'm part of the action. Hope I can handle my fifteen seconds of fame.

"Thanks. You've done a great job. The gala is fabulous." I raise my glass.

She raises hers and we clink. "To Christmas magic."

We both sip our drinks. She sports a pageant-worthy wave and slinks through the small crowd of people, making her rounds. Very strange toast, but I guess we all need a little magic in our lives. Tonight's enchanting, no matter what. Weird, I can't wait to get myself out of this uncomfortable situation, yet I'm happy I'm here, like someone turned me into a fairy-tale princess. Well, except for the fact the prince referred to me as a whore, and the evil queen's forcing me to face him again for her own sadistic pleasure. Yep, ripped right out of the pages of Mother Goose.

I shift my eyes around the room, trying to place Nick's position. Our eyes lock as if they're pulled together by some magnetic force. God, why can't things be different? Stupid comment aside, our paths move in opposite directions. If the road only converged somewhere, we might have a shot at being together. Ah, who am I kidding? It just was never meant to be.

His lips upturn to that irresistibly sexy smile. Oh God, I'm staring. I swing around toward the podium.

"Holly, you look stunning. Very nice to see you here. Are you enjoying the gala?" Mayor Whitman pops a stuffed mushroom into his mouth.

Didn't even realize the mayor knew my name. Guess I'm part of the in-crowd. "Yes, it's spectacular."

"We're lucky Nick is so fond of Hilldale. With his generous donations, we were able to be extra festive this year. His presence alone raised our fundraising over seventy percent. The library may even add another wing." He slugs a glass of champagne. "You've got a good man."

I smile and nod. What else can I do? At this point it's easier just to play the game for another thirty-five minutes.

I glance behind me. *Dammit.* Caught in his gaze yet again. I lower my focus to the floor. A vision of Nick coming closer moves into the corner of my eye.

"Have a lovely time, Mayor. Excuse me." I hightail it to the bathroom. Okay, not the most mature plan. Steering clear of him makes it easier on both of us. Plus this whole experience is awkward enough. No need to complicate things any more.

I take a quick glance in the mirror and adjust the blond curls of my up-do. The silver sparkles on the light blue fabric of the dress glisten like specks of fresh-fallen snow. I turn from side to side, trying to take in the princess aura flowing through me. Too bad there's always a catch.

I smack on some desert rose lipstick and grab my clutch. Can't hide in here forever. With my luck, someone will notice and figure I've gotten sick. No need to bring any more attention to myself. For the next twenty minutes, being invisible works best. Time to take my rightful place. I leave my sanctuary also known as the women's restroom and stand in the back of the room near an artificial Christmas tree. Wallflower works for me.

Nick's gaze burns through me. No need to try and catch a glimpse, his heavy stare is unmistakable. I fidget with my fingers, sipping the fresh glass of champagne I grabbed during my dash back here. If I don't stop drinking before the ceremony, I'll make an interesting presenter. I turn my body at just the right angle so I can see Nick through the mirrored snowflake on the wall. He focuses on me like I'm the only person in the room. Ironic, for all the times I wished he'd look at me like that, this time I want him to turn away. How ridiculous. It's like we're stalking each other in a silly lover's game. Except no one wins.

Michelle steps up to the podium and turns on the microphone. Thank God. There's a light at the end of the tunnel. Soon I'll have served my penance and can leave all of this behind me. Guess I should revel in the spotlight for the next few minutes. Then it's back to my old life.

She pats the mic lightly. "On behalf of the board, Mayor Whitman, Mr. Green and myself, thank you all for attending this year's Holiday Gala. It's been a very successful season because of all of you. Please give yourselves a round of applause."

The crowd roars into a symphony of clapping. I tap my fingers together around my champagne glass.

She clears her throat, quieting the crowd. "First, we'll

announce the winners of the silent auction." She hoists a new painting up on a stand.

Wait, that's the beautiful winter scene Nick and I were admiring at the carnival. Looks even better under the glow of the dim lights. It's almost as if every Christmas light in the painting brightens up the night.

"*Lakeside Christmas* has turned up the most donations. I'm proud to announce the winner of this piece is Nick Shaw." She slams her hands together over the mic, creating a thunderous rumble.

The crowd hoots and hollers. Nick waves a hand in the air and sweeps the crowd. Our eyes meet once again. He winks and raises his glass to me. I hold my glass to the air. Yep, congrats. You won yet another thing with your money. Guess I shouldn't be so harsh. It's perfect for his new home and it's all for charity. Good for him, he deserves the painting.

I listen to Michelle read off the rest of the silent auction winners, waiting for my turn to grace the stage. Nick's eyes burn through me. Might as well enjoy it, won't last much longer. Not like I'll be attending these types of soirees in the future. Time flies by quicker than anticipated, looks like I'm up. I pull the check out of my purse and nibble on my lip. Here goes nothing.

"I'd like to turn the stage over to Holly Clifford of Trust Realty." Michelle holds out the mic.

I march up to the stage, trying not to trip on the way. My heart races like a galloping stallion. I take a deep breath and take the mic from Michelle. My hand trembles during the exchange. I look out onto the crowd. Angie smirks, her arms folded over her chest, and the tip of her high heel taps on the floor. Great, she's dying for me to stumble.

I steady myself and swallow hard. I open my mouth to speak but nothing comes out. Oh God, I practiced this two-minute speech a million times. What's happening? My mind goes completely blank. I struggle for words but it's no use. A pearl of sweat forms on my hairline. *Come on, Holly, think.* I gaze around at the dozens of stares fixated on me. My eyes water. *Dear God, please don't let me cry.*

My eyes find Nick's and lock with them yet again. The warm caramel hue calms my nerves. I shift my focus and take in his vibe. Still nothing.

He sets down his glass and walks toward the podium. Oh God, what's he doing? I can't move a muscle. I'm sucked into the abyss of pure perfection coming closer with every second. Nick stands next to me and takes the mic from my hand.

"Sorry to interrupt, but this can't wait any longer." He turns toward me as if I'm the only person in the room.

Jeez. I embarrassed myself enough for one night. No need to give everyone more to talk about.

"If you haven't heard, I bought a house in Hilldale." The crowd claps for a few seconds. "Yep, I'm coming back during the off season, and our own Holly Clifford from Trust Realty made that happen for me."

Heat creeps across my face from my cheeks to my ears. Looks like the hero's saving the damsel in distress yet again. Thank God for heroes. A small smile forms.

"Pretty much every important event in my life happened here in Hilldale. Lots of firsts." He paces around and faces the crowd. "Fifth grade, Randy Jacobs brought his brother's Led Zeppelin IV CD over to my house after junior football practice. First time I heard those powerful vocals and intense riffs, my world changed. Now I blast it before every game."

Oh my God, the box. The one he left on my porch. It's all coming together.

"How about that blizzard about eight years back when the whole town shut down? That's when I sprained my wrist and couldn't join the snowball war. My sister left a copy of *The Stand* on our coffee table. TV was out and I was trapped inside so I gave it shot. First time I sat home and read a book. Never realized they transport you into a different world. After that I was hooked on Stephen King."

Okay, so the theory I concocted was a bit off. Why did he want to share all of these things with me? Was he expecting to bail me out tonight, or is there more to this master plan?

"And the muddy football from Hilldale High's state championship game. I still keep that on my desk, mud and all. That's the first time I realized how many people in this town stand behind me and how we all stick together."

Guess he's right. The one thing about Hilldale is that everyone has an unseen bond together. Maybe I'm part of the bond too. Could it have been me forsaking this town rather than the other way around?

"Even though I've lived here my whole life and there've been a lot of firsts for me here, this last two weeks beats them all." His tongue darts out, wetting his lips. "For the first time ever, I met a girl I can't get off my mind." He loosely grabs my fingers. "One who calls me out on my bullshit and who's more impressed with a stuffed polar bear than a diamond necklace."

My face erupts into an all-out smile. I glance at the crowd. They're smiling and staring in the same way Josie does, like they want me to finally get the happy ending.

Nick nibbles at his lip, muffling a smile. "I've met hundreds, maybe thousands of people, and the one thing I can say without a doubt, there's only one Holly Clifford and no one else even comes close. I've got to do whatever it takes to keep her, because nothing makes sense without her."

Lava flows through my veins. We stare into each other's eyes, lost in the moment. My pulse skyrockets. How could I stay away from Nick or write this town out of my life? Sure, there're a million obstacles and so much can go wrong, but sometimes the biggest risks reap amazing rewards. A tear streams down my face. Oh God, I need a second to think. I've got to get out of here. I drop the check and rush away through the crowd, snagging my shoe against one of the bistro tables. It flies from my foot but I keep trekking forward until I'm outside.

The cool, crisp air douses the flames running through me. After a few seconds I stop at the wooden gazebo encrusted in white lights. I close my eyes and take a deep breath, desperately trying to clear my head. What am I doing? I've got to go back and talk to Nick. I spin around to head back to the gala.

"You know, you're not in the enchanted forest. If you lose a shoe in Hilldale at midnight, you're probably drunk." Nick walks toward me, carrying my silver shoe, a sexy smile plastered across his face.

I chuckle. Amazing, he can make me smile at any given moment. "It's only nine o'clock."

"Then you're cut off." He bends down, setting my shoe on the ground. His eyes lock with mine. "I'm sorry. I was a jerk.... Forgive me?"

After what he just did? The moment he stepped up and grabbed the mic, all prior stupid comments from the past and present were absolved. I doubt anything for the rest of my existence will even come close to tonight. Ah, the most romantic moment ever, and it happened to me.

I nod. "What happens now?"

He slides the silver heel onto my foot. "Anything your heart desires. Oh, and we live happily ever after." He stands.

"I don't think it works like that." I nibble on my lip.

He lifts my chin. "Sky's the limit. Anything is possible." He lifts his eyes and points to the top of the gazebo. "Someone owes me a kiss."

A dangling bunch of mistletoe hangs from the center of the lighted structure. A split second later, snow flurries fall from the sky. I swear the sound of sleigh bells resonates in the distance. It's like we're in the middle of a snow globe capturing this moment.

I wrap my arms around Nick's neck. "Just one?"

"For now. We'll figure it out as we go." He presses his lips against mine.

I close my eyes and see a future I never imagined, one that I can't live without. I weave my fingers through the back of Nick's hair and pour all the passion I feel into this one perfect kiss. Anything is possible, especially with Nick Shaw by my side. I'm a believer. Christmas magic exists.

MEET THE AUTHOR

Amy L. Gale

Romance author by night, pharmacist by day, Amy L. Gale loves rock music and the feel of sand between her toes. She attended Wilkes University where she graduated with a Doctor of Pharmacy degree. In addition to writing, she enjoys baking, scary movies, rock concerts, and reading books at the beach. She lives in the lush forest of Northeastern Pennsylvania with her husband, six cats, and golden retriever.

OTHER TITLES FROM

5 PRINCE PUBLISHING